NAUTICAL NIGHTMARES

NAUTICAL NIGHTMARES

This book is for entertainment purposes only.

Library of Congress Control Number: 2024938436

Printed in United States of America

ISBN: 9798894670003

Table of Contents

Phins

S.W. Salzman

The *ping* sounded across the cabin.

Kirsten's eyes fluttered from the chair she was kicked back in. Other than a grunt and a quick snore, that was about it.

Ping... ping...

Her eyes shot open. She leapt from her chair and rushed to the sonar. After five days adrift in the middle of the South Pacific with nothing other than the occasional blip of a school of mackerel or a rogue shark, the prospect of a new encounter– a *real* one this time– sent a tinge of excitement throughout her core.

Five green blips appeared on the screen. They were large, much bigger than a school of fish, and these weren't moving; Her vessel was moving toward them. Kirsten shifted sideways to the control panel and checked the monitors. The wind speed was a near-constant eighteen kilometers per hour. She took note of that as she ran calculations in her head. Judging by the size of her research vessel, *The Wayward Soul*, and figuring in the wind speed, she estimated the ship was drifting at a little over two knots.

Ping... ping...

According to the sonar, the vessel had drifted to within a half-kilometer of the mysterious objects. The possibilities swirled within her mind of what could be out there waiting for them. Without another moment's hesitation, she scurried down the short flight of steps to the sleeping quarters.

"Mique," she called out as she hit the bottom step.

He didn't make a peep, didn't even flinch.

She shook him. *Nada.* She stared at his sleeping form with that same irritated look his conscious form grew to know so well. He didn't want to wake up? That was fine. She pinched his nose and held his mouth shut.

"Mique," she growled. "Get up, you turd."

It didn't take more than a few seconds. Mique's eyes popped open as he flailed his arms and jerked his head free, gasping for breath.

"Damn, girl," Mique chided. "The hell you trying to do, kill me?"

"Next time, listen to me." She shrugged, then slapped him on the arm. "Get your butt up and come up top. We found something dead ahead."

Mique's eyes widened, this time out of excitement instead of terror. He leapt from the bed, wearing only his boxers and a white tee. Getting dressed crossed his mind, but there would be time for that later.

"Damn, girl," Mique said, shaking his head. "Why didn't you just say so?"

"*Damn girl, damn girl*...is that all you can say?" she said, mocking him.

"Damn, girl," he teased with a huge grin. "You're touchy."

Kirsten just rolled her eyes and followed after him.

Mique took a glance at the sonar, more to make sure she wasn't full of shit, then walked out onto the forward deck and gazed out at the black waters dappled with specks of moonlight. Hand to this forehead, he scanned the waters.

This time, Kirsten rolled her eyes and shook her head. Every time he did that, it pissed her off and he knew it. But seeing how worked up he could get her was always a great time.

"What do you see out there, genius?" Kirsten's voice settled into less-than-enthusiastic.

"Water," he said, grinning. "Lots and lot of water."

"You're a jackass," she barked back.

"I think we should send down the ROV," Mique said. "Did we ever get the night vision fixed on it?"

"Duh," she said with an exaggerated nod. "Lucas and I did that before we left port."

"Oh, yeah," said Mique, doing his best Butthead impersonation.

"You're a turd." Kirsten walked away.

"Get Lucas up and get the ROV ready," Mique called after her.

She flipped him off over her shoulder.

Lucas peered into the water. The ROV's green LED blinked back at him, and he was assured it was ready for its mission.

He took a seat at the monitor with its green glowing view of the water before it as white specs of salt and a few strings of fish shit floated past.

"Number two," Mique regarded him. "Make it so."

"Yes, sir," Lucas huffed, then said under his breath, "Captain Jean Luc Fucktard."

Mique's eyes shot daggers when Kirsten snort-laughed. She rushed a hand up to cover her mouth.

"Let's just do this," Mique said, barely above a whisper.

The near-silent whoosh of the small twin propellers fed from the speakers as the small vessel glided along. Lucas thumbed the twin joysticks. The ROV (Remote Operated Vehicle) drifted to the right, although from their perspective, its direction never changed. Their only sense of direction came from a small display of latitude and longitude in the lower right corner of the monitor.

Lucas hurried a glance behind at Kirsten. "Where are we supposed to be looking again?" Kirsten read the coordinates at the bottom of the monitor, then the sonar. She compared them to the map on the table.

She answered in play-by-play as she traced the route on the map. "It looks like... if you keep heading along the same coordinates... the blips should be—"

"Holy fucking shit!" Lucas shouted with excitement. "Get a load of this shit!"

Mique leaned in, his chin practically resting on Lucas's

shoulder. "Is that what I think it is?"

Kirsten rushed over and pointed at the screen. "Holy fuck! That's a pod of—"

"Sperm whales," Lucas finished her sentence.

"One... two...," Mique began to count.

"Six of 'em," Kirsten beat him to the punch. "That's creepy as shit."

Six massive sperm whales hung vertically in the drift about one hundred fifty feet below the surface. Arranged in a sort of circular shape, a juvenile not much more than twenty feet slumbered in the center, flanked by its much larger familial unit, which included a massive bull. From the vantage point of the three on the ship, the bull had to be close to sixty-five feet long—a fear-inducing gargantuan of the ocean.

"I can't believe we found some," Mique was astonished. "We've been on this project for our entire summer break, and now—"

Lucas interrupted. "And now I'm scared shitless. I mean, look at them."

"A pod of sleeping sperm whales," Kirsten grew more excited with each word. "Can you imagine what the university will think? There haven't been many studies on the sleeping habits of sperm whales. Most of what scientists know has been nothing but speculation. If we can take *Hilda* in close and—"

"Are you crazy?" Lucas gave a hurried head shake. "We can't take *Hilda* into the middle of those things! If we disturb them, we're fucked."

Mique nodded. "I'm sorry, Kirstie. Lucas is right. If we wake them, you can kiss two people and a two-million-dollar submersible goodbye. We should just use the ROV. That's not as much of a loss."

Hilda was a small, two-person HOV (Human Occupied Vehicle) similar to the *Triton 1000* submersible. It basically looked like two pontoons attached to an oversized bumper car with a thick Lexan glass canopy and a cockpit capable of holding two people side-by-side rather comfortably. It was extremely silent and maneuverable, capable of diving to depths of up to 320 meters, or a little over 1000 feet. It was perfect for mid-to-shallow-depth research.

"I can do it," Kirsten countered. "For chrissakes, Mique, this is the opportunity of a lifetime!"

"It's too risky." Mique shook his head.

Kirsten wasn't having it. "Dammit, I've been piloting a sub since before I learned how to drive a car. I know I can do it! I could steer *Hilda* through a feeding frenzy of great whites and never get a scratch!"

Mique pointed to the monitor. "Yeah, but one of *those* goddamned things so much as wakes up and swings its tail at that sub, and you'll be dead before you even know what hit you."

Kirsten shrugged. "Good thing Lucas is coming with me, then. I need a co-pilot."

"The fuck I am." Lucas looked at her like she was crazy.

Kirsten stared hard at them. "Look...guys. This is a once-in-a-lifetime opportunity. Think of the knowledge we could take back to the university with this. We'd be celebrated. And if we do this and I feel at any point that something is wrong or that we aren't safe, I will turn around and haul ass back to this ship, and we will use the ROV."

Lucas and Mique exchanged looks with one another, then back at her. Lucas half-shrugged and nodded to Mique.

Mique took a deep breath and held it as he stared at Kirsten. Finally, he exhaled and nodded. "Alright, let's take *Hilda* swimming."

Water covered the Lexan glass bubble as *Hilda* lowered beneath the surface and began her descent. Lucas sat shotgun and watched over the monitors and gauges as Kirsten opened the ballasts, triggered the throttle, and sent the sub into a gradual dive.

"All good down there?" Mique's voice popped over the radio.

"Good to go," Lucas replied.

"Alright." Mique nodded at no one. "Be careful."

"Will do, boss," Lucas answered.

Lucas flipped a switch, and the fore and aft lights kicked on. The ocean lit up around them in a thirty-foot radius. Past the radius was nothing but unforgiving black.

"Go slow," Lucas said evenly. "We don't want to wake them up."

Kirsten exhaled, then nodded. "Coordinates?"

Lucas checked the sonar. "Thirty-five meters, give or take a few."

She slowed almost to a stop.

"Turn off the sonar," she instructed him. "We don't want the ping to wake them. We're gonna have to inch in blind."

Lucas made the sign of the cross.

"What the hell was that?" Kirsten smiled at him. "You don't

believe in God."

Lucas's eyes widened. "Tonight, I do."

Less than a minute later, the slumbering behemoths appeared through the glass. Lucas and Kirsten both shivered in unison at the sight of the beautifully frightening creatures. "Fuck me," Lucas was awestruck.

The sub hovered just below eye level of the giant cetaceans.

Kirsten feathered the throttle. The sub inched forward.

"Okay, get the arm out with the sensor," she said as she chewed her lip. "Once we get within a foot, activate the sensor. It should guide itself and attach."

"Whale EKG is ready to roll," Lucas affirmed.

The giant whale visibly shuddered. Then the eye popped open; its pupil instantly dilated from the light.

Kirsten screamed inwardly as she killed the throttle.

After an eternal second, the eye fluttered and closed.

Lucas swallowed hard. "I think I shit myself."

Kirsten's face scrunched. "Don't make me make you get out and swim."

"Don't make me make you get out and swim," he parroted and rolled his eyes, pitching his voice into a reedy, petulant whine.

Back to business, Kirsten inched the sub forward.

The arm hovered dangerously close to the thick skin. They were close enough to see the fine hairs sway with the mild current.

"Now," she whispered.

Lucas pressed a switch and released the arm. The sensor whirred and embedded itself into the whale's hide.

"Damn, girl," Mique's whisper came through. "That was fucking sick! We're getting readings. Come on back."

Kirsten held her breath, then exhaled, relieved. "On our way."

She reversed the sub until they were about fifteen meters, then was about to turn around when Mique's voice spiked over the speaker.

"Kirsten," Mique called, urgent. "There are three blips on the screen. They're closing in fast—thirty-five knots. Get the hell out of there before they—"

That's when they saw them—bio-luminescent eyes shooting through the water like rockets, headed straight for the bull sperm whale. The black silhouettes just past the reach of the sub's light bobbed as they swam, like—

"Are those dolphins?" Lucas stared wide-eyed.

"They can't be," Kirsten hurried a reply. "They're far too

big."

Out of the blackness, one of the incoming things burst into view. It *looked* like a dolphin, yet not. It was almost twenty feet long from first perception and black as the night sea. But its eyes... the eyes were bio-luminescent, glowing like a violet phosphor.

"Jesus Christ!" Lucas freaked out. "Get us the fuck out of here."

The bull sperm whale's eye burst open in a panic. It thrust its tail and flipped itself horizontal, its eyes trained on the sub.

"Fuck... fuck! FUCK!"

Kirsten hammered the throttle. The sub shot backward just as the bull flailed its mighty tail. Its head lunged forward as its mouth went agape, exposing a palate of twenty-one-centimeter teeth. Lucas covered his head and screamed.

The mouth was about to swallow the sub whole.

Then the gargantuan's eyes widened. A deafening scream erupted as the black dolphin-like creature slammed into its side just as another rushed from the shadows and slammed its beak-like nose into the whale's eye, sending globules of ruined eye tissue into the water as it turned red.

The remaining pod members thrashed in a panic and scattered. The adolescent trailed behind them.

Their panic proved fatal.

A third dolphin-like creature smashed into the adolescent. Its fourteen-centimeter teeth sunk into its flesh and tore its right flipper from its body. Ruined, the adolescent succumbed to a relentless repeat attack as its life and internal organs spilled into the frigid ocean waters.

Mique screamed over the radio, "What the fuck is going on down there?"

Kirsten slammed her hand on the mic. "I don't know! They're—they're like dolphins, but they're huge! They're larger than great whites!"

"They're black as night," Lucas roared into the mic. "And they got these fucking glowing eyes!"

Mique wracked his brain, whisking through his mind. Finally, it came to him. "*Cephalorhynchus*!"

"They can't be," Kirsten called back. "They're too fucking big!"

Fuck, this could be the fucking find of the century, Mique thought excitedly.

Then Mique lost his fucking mind.

"Turn on the video," he ordered. "Get in there and get

pictures! We need to document this!"

"Fuck you, asshole!" Lucas yelled. "You're outta your goddamned– JESUS FUCKING CHRIST!!"

The head of the bull filled their viewpoint as it shot toward them. Kirsten slammed the throttle and yanked the stick.

The sub veered left just as the bull shot past. Its tail whisked and clipped the right ballast, sending the sub– and its screaming occupants– into a dizzying spin.

The bull crashed into the hull, rupturing the fuel tank, and The Wayward Soul exploded. Mique was dead before he even realized what happened.

The concussive force eviscerated the bull's head. Its corpse began to sink while the black predators rushed in to devour it.

Kirsten gunned the throttle, but the sub was listing badly from the damaged ballast. She had to constantly fiddle with the stick to keep the craft moving in a steady forward motion.

"This thing is fucked." Lucas was aghast as he continuously stole nervous glances behind at the carnage.

"All we have to do is make it to the surface." Kirsten took a deep breath.

Lucas could see the glow of the flaming wreckage. It looked like the sun beneath the water. "Poor Mique," he whispered.

"Fuck Mique," Kirsten countered. "He only gave a shit about himself."

Lucas stabbed the comm button and spun the frequency dial. "Coast Guard, this is Lucas aboard the *Hilda* Triton-class sub. Can you—"

"Forget it, Lucas," Kirsten shook her head. "There's no outside comms. This is direct freq only."

Lucas slammed his fist on the console. "God fucking dammit!"

"Stay calm," Kirsten said more for herself than him. "We're almost to the surface. We'll pop the top and send a flare."

No sooner did the sub breach the surface than a whoosh erupted, followed by the Lexan glass top's ejection into the water.

Kirsten snatched the flare gun from the emergency kit, aimed high, and fired. The bright, fluorescent pink explosion lit up the sky.

She nodded at Lucas.

He sighed. "What do we do now?"

"We wait," Kirsten shrugged.

They turned back to the wreckage. Black smoke plumed into

the sky as the flames kissed the water.

"What the fuck are those things?"

Kirsten had no clue. "I don't know. New species, maybe?"

"Those eyes," Lucas shook his head. "They were—"

"So eerie and unnatural," She finished his sentence this time.

"This could change everything," Lucas was thoughtful. "A new apex predator. We have to tell the university when we make it back."

She nodded. "*If* we make it back."

"No, no, no," Lucas corrected her. "Don't you do that. We're gonna make it back."

"I'm sorry," Kirsten looked defeated. "I should have listened to you both."

"Not your fault," Lucas assured her. "We didn't know those things were down there."

She bit her lower lip. "I guess not."

A protracted silence stretched between them.

Lucas closed his eyes, shook his head. "What they did to that whale... Fuck. You don't think they will come after us, do you?"

"I don't know."

"I hope n—"

The water geysered as the black torpedo breached. Before the two could even register it, the thing arced over the sub. Its jaws closed around Lucas in a sickening crunch. His piercing scream echoed out, then fell silent as the black demon splashed back into the water, taking Lucas with it.

Blood splashed across Kirsten's face. She screamed for what seemed an eternity, until she slumped down in the open cockpit and sobbed. She now had no choice but to believe in God as Lucas did. She whispered a desperate prayer that the Coast Guard would find her. She felt hopeless.

She was alone.

She was terrified.

And she was prey.

S.W. Salzman is an accomplished audiobook narrator, voice and screen actor, musician and writer. When he is not writing or working on other projects, expect to find him out in nature on adventures big and small (usually hiking or at the local library or bookstore), attending concerts and music festivals, on the water, around a bonfire or having a backyard barbeque.

He is the author of The Final Day: The Full 24 Hours and co-author of Hellbenders among others. He currently resides in southern Wisconsin with his children and his cat, Tormund.

This Godforsaken Barge

Cheyanne Brabo

When my first crewmate fused with the ship's steel wall, I knew we'd made a mistake in trying to cross Lake Superior.

In the early night, as the worst storm of 1950 raged around our lumber barge, I found myself dashing below deck to the source of a massive sound. The noise, the shrieking scream of mangled metal, was loud enough to hear over the roaring sound of the violent wind and crashing waves.

Like all of us, I could scarcely comprehend what I saw as I turned into the ship's messroom. All I knew was that Roger was crying, and I could only see a quarter of his body.

Aaron, a huge man playing impromptu chef that night, came rushing to Roger's aid as I stood with my mouth hanging open in the stairway. Only Roger's head, hands, shins and knees were visible to me; the rest of his body had been absorbed into the metal behind him. Though I couldn't understand what I was looking at, blood was beginning to dribble from Roger's purple and blue-tinged lips, and it was obvious that the wall had cut through his neck.

With his eyes swiveling around the room desperately, Roger coughed out a wet gurgle. Aaron and I hardly had time to react before his big brown eyes glazed over in asphyxiation.

"Good Lord in Heaven!" I heard the gruff voice of our Captain calling from behind us.

"Holy shit!" Aaron yelled, wiping sweat from his bright red face. "What in the hell?"

On the upper deck, over the ever-angry waters of Lake Superior, the wind howled like an injured animal. As the room listed to the right as our vessel roared over furious waves, everyone in the messroom squatted and leaned to keep themselves upright. Roger's arms and legs leaned with the ship too, grotesquely limp as he hung on the wall.

Captain Osborn stomped across the hardwood floor, bracing himself against the Roger-infused wall as he came to investigate. When the terrible, shrieking sound called out around us again, we tried to ignore it before Captain Osborn himself began screaming too. In the ugly orange light of the messroom, I watched the Captain's hand pass into the metal wall only inches away from Roger's head.

Our Captain was a stoic, serious man, an elderly seaman with a graying beard, years of experience, and a bad attitude to boot. I'd never heard him yell unless he was raising his voice to give an order, but on that horrific night, the Captain screamed like a wiped dog.

Instantly, my shipmates piled around him, grabbing onto the old man's hips and shoulders, trying desperately to yank him out of the steel. The Captain himself was fighting like an animal in a trap and as I yelled for someone to get back on the ship's wheel, I thought the Captain was about to rip his own hand off.

The room itself fell into chaos, hysterical voices echoing around the messroom as we tried to understand what was happening. "Richard!" I yelled, calling my Captain by his first name, trying to get through to him, "You have to calm down! You're gonna hurt yourself!"

"I can't calm down, damn it!" Captain Osborn yelled back. "Chambers just ran up the stairs – that boy is gonna steer us into the lake, and I'm stuck in the Goddamned wall!"

Before I could say another word, as if the water itself had overheard Captain Osborn, the entire ship rolled violently as it made impact with another wave.

My feet left the hardwood floor, and I flew across the room as the ship struck the water with all the force of a car crash. Into one of the dining tables I went, my shoulder smashing on impact. Pain engulfed my left side as the ship swung right, and I rolled across the floor accordingly. The Captain was hollering all the while, his voice cracking with the force of his terror. "Get me out of here! Get me out of this wall, God damn it!"

I righted myself on my hands and knees, crawling like a toddler as I peered around the tousled room. Though I'd successfully bounced off the furniture, three other men had been absorbed into the metal walls like flies in a tar pit. Throbbing pain arched like molten fire through my left arm as I tried to make sense of the scene around me, the pained shrieks of my shipmates like the tormented souls of hell.

Torsos with no heads and bodies cut vertically through solid ship steel hung like demonic taxidermy as the storm roared around us. God Himself seemed hellbent on proving that we had no business on Lake Superior in the middle of this storm. The lightning itself seemed angry, infused with the wrath of God, as it trapped five grown men in the walls of our lumber barge.

Not for the first time that night, I wished we'd never boarded that God-forsaken barge. If Captain Osborn hadn't called that morning with the promise that we could sell lumber on the American side of the lake for thrice the usual price, I would've listened to my wife and stayed home with my family. Either way, the barge was being thrown around the water like a child's toy as I watched men thrash and scream with their limbs contorted like tortured dolls.

Like a boom of thunder falling over me, I remembered that with the Captain trapped in the mess room, Chambers was still steering our ship. Captain Osborn was right – letting Chambers steer was like leaving the ship in the hands of an incompetent child.

Up the stairs I scrambled, the ship moaning around me as my crewmates bellowed. Water was coming down the staircase as I hiked up it, the essence of the lake rolling off the deck. I could hear the massive chains which secured the lumber to the deck being shaken like windchimes. Spare twigs and bunches of leaves were flying around my head at tornado speed.

On the open deck, driving rain came spraying across my face as a bolt of lightning shot out of the blackened sky above me. Bright light came arching down, impacting the metal directly behind me as the ship's hull imitated another terrible screech. As I jumped away from the arching bolt, I thought I saw something black and massive in the thunderhead above, something familiar and furious. I went dashing across the open deck regardless, trying not to pay attention to what I couldn't change.

The small, exposed wheelhouse was composed of a glass

room with a flimsy wooden door that did little to shield me as another bolt of lightning pierced the wooden beam next to my head.

"Holy shit!" Chambers yelled, as soon as the bolt and I entered the room, "What the hell is going on? Where's Richard? What's happening down there?"

Bracing myself against the wall, I watched massive waves slam into the ship's bow, the midsized vessel listing as Chambers attempted to steer us safely in the angry water. He was a young, wily man, no older than twenty, his child's face pulled into an expression of desperation and panic. I rushed to his side, my hands over his as I helped attempt to keep us all out of harm's way.

He wiggled away from the wheel, dripping in sweat as he backed away from me. "We're gonna die," he told me in a quiet, certain voice, "We're gonna die out here. We never should've left land."

I didn't answer him; I didn't have the nerve to. All my focus had shifted to keeping our barge above water. As a massive swell broke across the ship, spraying sheets of water across the window in front of me, the great shouting of steel and metal screeched out once more. The inexplainable electric phenomenon afflicting us, the divine retribution of the water itself was at work. I kept my eyes glued to the water in front of me as the entire room seemed to shrink.

When the ship quieted, the shrill shrieking sound continued, and it took me several long moments to realize that it was my own voice yelling.

With one fleeting glance, I saw that I'd sunk to my knees into the steel floor below me. Only the fiberglass ceiling of the messroom was preventing me from falling all the way through the deck. I couldn't see Chambers behind me, but judging from the intensity of his screams, I guessed he was none the better.

I couldn't stop the sounds from crawling from my mouth, could hardly see through my tear-blurred vision. Never could I have imagined how horrible the pain would be. Searing agony shot up my calves and through the veins in my thighs like liquified flame.

With all the resolve left inside of me, I steered on, attempting to hit the roiling water as softly as I could. Screaming into the night, I could do nothing but watch as one final wave crested over the entire ship, a wall of water eighty feet high engulfing all the metal and wood on which we depended. Beneath us, I heard the constant hum of the boat's engine stop as it drowned in lake water.

Fused in place behind the wheel as the storm continued to rage around us, I knew that our barge had taken on too much water to recover. The entire vessel listed forward, as the weight of logs older than my grandfather sent us sinking faster into the inky, angry lake.

I found myself wishing that I'd been frozen through the wall in the mess room, that the ship's metal had gone through my middle and killed me before I came into the wheelhouse.

Not only was I frozen to the floor, an impromptu Captain for the final moments of my life, but I could see the monster thunderhead in its entirety through the glass ahead. In the black clouds, illuminated only by the constant crack of lightning, I could see two massive, blackened eyes and an angry, opened mouth – a face staring down at us—God come to condemn us at last.

With the entire crew trapped in the walls of the vessel, God will send us to the bottom of Lake Superior slowly, sinking us gently so that we know the magnitude of our sins as we join all the other capsized men whose greed convinced them that they were greater than the wrath of this Godforsaken lake.

Cheyanne Brabo (she/her) is a queer fiction writer from Northern California. Her work appears in Scissor Sisters Sapphic Villain's Anthology, Broken Olive Branches, Warning Lines Lit, and Moth Eaten Mag, and was a finalist in Crystal Lake Entertainment's Flash Fiction Contest. When she's not writing, she enjoys taking her cat on leash walks. Find her on Twitter @cheysectoplasm.

Hold Your Breath

C. P. Swift

Nobody ever comes out to the old aquarium, so when I hear footsteps crunching on the shellrock path, I quit tossing palm nuts into the ocean and just watch. The visitor looks a little bit like those blond, long-legged dolls I used to play with—same blank face and all.

Nobody ever comes out here, so when she slips inside the abandoned building, I can't help but follow her.

I walk softly, so she can't hear my sneakers on the thin, salt-ravaged carpet.

Hands on hips, backpack on back, she surveys the stained walls and broken fixtures, looking like an astronaut who has just landed on the moon.

I have a backpack, too. Maybe that means I'm like her.

"Hi," I say, painting my chin with the dark end of my braid.

I was hoping to scare her, but when she turns around I can see she's too businessy to be easily scared.

"Hello," she says, not warmly, just politely. I understand polite; Mama taught me that.

"What are you doing?" I also understand rude, which is asking too many questions, but I do it anyway.

"I just bought this place. There's a lot of work to be done."

Together, we scan the building's gutted, reeking insides. The way she talks, I wonder if she can see it the way it used to look before the accident. I remember the orange-bright counters. Wall-to-ceiling aquariums swelling with sea life. Little strings of lights giving it a magical, otherworldly glow. Now it's heavy with the smells of dead fish, mildew and loss. But it doesn't hurt to remember.

"Are you going to make it nice again?" I ask.

But she has already left me and is running her fingers over the seal on one of the dead tanks. It's not the one that broke.

I reach out again for her attention. "Aren't you afraid of the ghosts?"

"There's no such thing as ghosts," she says, and on the tail end of the sentence, "This one's not too bad. I wonder which pump goes to it."

Even frowning and muttering to herself, she's so pretty. My sneakered feet eagerly follow hers to a room marked "mechanical." I'm so close behind her that when she turns around, she startles. I grin.

"Don't you have a tablet to play on or something?"

I hate when grown-ups say that, but I'm used to it. Reaching into my bag, I pull it out and show her.

"Where are your parents, anyway?"

"I live just down the beach. Can I please stay?"

She points. "You can stand in the doorway."

I do as I'm told while she pushes aside the cobwebs shrouding the machinery and kicks aside the ruined things on the floor—life jackets that no one had time to get to, scuba equipment that might have saved someone. The smell of damp and chemicals tickles my nose. She squints at labels in the heavy air and finally turns some valves, flicks some switches. A low whine sharpens until I have to cover my ears. When I hear a splashing over my shoulder, I jump.

She's smiling. "It worked!"

When she squeezes past me, I catch a scent of citrus.

"It's going to take awhile," she comments, watching the water spill into the enormous tank. The sound is like a small waterfall and underneath it, a groaning and shuddering make my teeth vibrate.

"It's okay," she says, her sharp blue gaze capturing my wide brown one. "It's just the pipes."

We wait on a musty step covered with thin, peeling carpet. I feel the warmth of her next to me. I remember that feeling.

"A lot of animals died here," I tell her. "A lot of people, too. They couldn't get away and they drowned." I don't tell her Mama was one of them. Already, the light seeping in is taking on the fuzzy blue-gray quality of dusk. I poke at the toe of my sneaker. "That's why people don't come anymore."

"They'll come when I'm done with it," she says cheerfully. "I'm going to turn it into a sealife center for animals to go to when they retire. Here, look."

She shows me a picture on her phone. It's of her wearing the same ponytail and a wetsuit. She's dangling a fish over a pool while a dolphin leaps for it. she takes the phone back, and smiles at the photo for a second before swiping it away.

"Cool," I say. I want to reach for her hand, but don't let myself. I'm starting to feel that funny, scary feeling the darker it gets. Glancing up at the skylights, I can already spot a few spiteful stars.

The splashing hums in my bloodstream. The clangs of the pipes bite my nerves. In front of me, water sloshes in the tank, a great green monster slowly rising up.

Then it starts. The sounds that aren't water or pipes or pumps. The muffled chatter of sea mammals long gone. The whispers of people. Sighs. The unsuspecting giggles of small children.

She has gone still. "Do you hear that?"

"No," I say, tasting salt.

She's on her feet now, ready to take action. That's one of the things I like about her. Mama gave up so easily. She closed her eyes and just let the water take her.

The clicking starts. The first time I heard it, I didn't know what it was either. Electrical sparks? Dolphin chatter?

Now I know.

She's not looking so businessy now. She is doing that thing grown-ups do where they stand still and wait for more information before they make a decision. She's not going to like the information she gets. I lay my cheek on my knees.

People don't realize how powerful water is. People think they can get out, but water is fast. When it is set free, water, like gas, chokes. When it is angry, water, like rock, breaks. Water doesn't take pity on you. It's unforgiving.

"The tanks," she whispers.

She has finally noticed. It is not just the one tank filling up with water. As blue/blackness descends from above, sickly green rises up from below. It's all around us. Even the broken tanks swell and churn. Mended, they rise like leviathans, floor to ceiling, millions of tons of water silently screaming against glass.

And the clicking noise? It's not really clicking.

A tiny diamond appears in the largest tank. It becomes a lightning bolt. Each click breathes more life into the crack, until fingers of water poke through and trickle down the side.

She is smart. She runs for the door. I notice how she doesn't even grab for me. Maybe she doesn't have children, so she doesn't know that when there is danger, you are supposed to take us with you.

It doesn't matter. The door is shut and it won't open. She grunts and tugs for nothing.

The water doesn't explode into the room like it did that day. Instead it just rises. It is up to her elbows as I slosh towards her. Water pours from my nose, running warm as blood down my face. By the time I reach her, both our sneakers are churning in green.

I am not made of this world, and I am not made of the other, and because of it, I am heavy.

I throw my arms around her, and together we sink.

She fights to push me off. I try not to let it hurt my feelings. I don't belong to her after all. She doesn't owe me anything.

It is only underwater that I realize how truly different they are. Her floating ponytail is a straw-colored mass. Mama's hair floated around her head in a dark halo. Her eyes are twin sapphires of terror. Mama's were lidded and sleepy. Mama's spirit was peaceful as she smiled and let go of my hands, slipping easily off to that other place, leaving me behind.

I didn't know to hold on, but this time I know better.

I will hold on. I will not let go.

I cinch my arms more tightly around her waist, smaller than Mama's waist. I lay my cheek against her chest, also smaller, harder. Her lungs heave as she holds her breath longer than she is supposed to. I close my eyes and pretend.

There's nothing peaceful about how she goes. Her scent of citrus is not Mama's honeysuckle shampoo.

It's not the same. I knew it wouldn't be.

It's not really what I want.

But it will have to be enough.

C.P. Swift is a science-fiction and fantasy author who loves to write about sweeping worlds and human (and nonhuman) connection, usually with a touch of the paranormal. Her novel, PLANET OF SOULS, is currently on submission with Bonnie Swann at The Purcell Agency. Her epic fantasy, SHARDS OF POWER, based on the board game Rolling Empires, is available free at www.royalroad.com.

Chasing Whales

Bert Lestrange

The ocean, both vast and immeasurable, has always been a mystery to our species. A finite, yet seemingly endless world as alien as outer space. It remains a mostly unexplored frontier, calling to the adventurous and bold. A plane of undulating shadows and mysterious whispers, ancient secrets lie beneath its depths.

One such secret found us purely by accident.

While scanning the seafloor for new forms of eel, my wife, the illustrious Marine Biologist Dr. Trisha Clark, happened to catch a glimpse of one of nature's most curious sights—an extinct species. Not just the one, but a pod of Balaenoptera molles. While fossils have been found, none before her has documented a sighting in recorded history.

Imagine her excitement and trepidation as she reported her findings from the depths below. It had always been her dream to find and name a new species. While this one had a proper name, its common name was still up in the air. Should we document its existence, we may very well have the Clark's Whale on our hands.

"They're about to breach!" were her last words.

Understanding immediately, I rushed for the armory, which is what we called our arsenal of tagging devices. There was only one among them that might suffice. I had one shot at this and made it count.

The modified spear gun sent a thin shaft into the back of the first to surface. It felt nothing, even as I reeled in the bolt's hollow body.

When Trisha surfaced, she moved immediately to the control room. The grin on my face mirrored her own enthusiasm. I pointed to a faintly blinking blip on the radar. "We got him!"

That sparked enough funding to procure a state-of-the-art exploratory vessel, a handful of crew to guide her, and a space-age miniature submarine. Thus, we began our search, which spanned the last two months.

The tracking device functioned like any other GPS; however, when the whales dove too deep, the beacon became untraceable. It was a game of cat and mouse on a global scale, but we ventured on with clear purpose and iron determination.

Imagine our elation when the signal boomed bright and clear, remaining in the same approximate location for several days.

We arrived in one of the loneliest places on earth. Point Nemo. It was the farthest one could be from land while remaining within Earth's atmosphere. Cold, isolated, and feral winds that cut to the bone, stealing anything not lashed to the side. After three days of brutal swells and ravaging gales, we had a brief enough respite to facilitate our descent into the unknown.

The captain bid us Godspeed over the com, and down we went into an eerie blackness without compare. Deep ocean held a singular isolation unlike any other. At least in the infinite void of space, there were stars to keep one company. Down here, we had only ourselves and the beams of our floodlights. Even those faded, the gravity of billions of gallons of seawater crushing down around us, swallowing it up like a ravenous leviathan.

At nearly two-thousand fathoms, the first signs of the ocean floor began to appear.

Until this point, we'd seen no sign of life; not even coral grew so far down. Yet as our lights skimmed, new points of radiance shimmered into existence.

Strange creatures appeared, then disappeared, before our viewing ports. A galaxy of jellyfish swam with curious glowing patterns, with body shapes completely foreign to the rational shallows. They drifted, some like fractals, others like drops of ink scattered in a bowl of water. Fish, too, great fanged maws loomed with lantern-like appendages dangling before them.

That might have been enough to suit an average biologist—but we had a specific goal in mind.

Imagine our shock and curiosity when the first spires of a ruined civilization rose before us.

Ancient stone clearly worked even after centuries, possibly millennia, of wear. Massive structures, carved with runes and sigils of no language either of us had seen before, each taller than a man.

Some of the structures were octagonal in nature, others simply stark, tall needles of stone. No vegetation grew, not down here. None of the weird creatures came within a hundred yards of it, but the beacon told us our whales were within.

While Trish steered, I snapped photo evidence, hardly daring to believe what we were seeing was real.

I was partway through another picture, when I realized the scale of the place. It must have been built by giants. The doors alone towered above the reach of our light field.

What forgotten civilization could have built such a necropolis? What terrible people had such technology so long ago?

"Is this Atlantis?" Trish whispered.

I shook my head, still enthralled by the sights. "In theory, Atlantis was a human society. Whatever species built this place could have crushed us beneath their heels. We would have been rats to them."

She was so caught up in the search for the whales that she hadn't noticed our instruments losing their metric. The compass spun wildly, and our readings of temperature, current direction, and depth were impossible to decipher.

As we closed, the readings indicated our quarry had entered a looming, circular formation of stone that looked for all the world to be a mighty, spined nautilus shell. Its golden ratio swirled in ever-shrinking circles, spiraling well above our range of vision. Like a gaping wound, an entrance, wide enough for an average home, loomed.

"I think they're inside." She whispered.

Unsure, I noticed the crazed dials for the first time. "Are you sure? How can you tell? The electronics are going wild."

While everything else whirled in disarray, external thermometer bouncing between 999 and −999 spasmodically, the tracking software held true.

She pointed to it, tapping the screen. "We've circled this place three times, and it continues pointing here. If we're going to find them, I think we must go inside."

"Is it safe? One minor mistake could be the end of us." I offered, hoping to sound more reasonable than terrified.

She nodded with a bravery I couldn't dream of matching. "Yes. I'll take her in slow with every precaution."

Turning to me with a glint of hope in her eyes, the same look I'd fallen in love with more than a decade before, she asked without asking. There was nothing I could refuse those eyes.

"If this is how it ends, I'd have it be this way: together and doing what we love."

She held my hand, smiling thanks that language couldn't properly express.

After a long moment, she returned to the joystick, and we ventured into the belly of the beast.

Whatever resemblance to a natural structure the exterior held, the interior was clearly manufactured. Giant runes were carved into the wall, but upon closer inspection, each was made of lesser symbols, and those even smaller. It wasn't safe to get closer than we already were, but it was obvious the pattern continued. Never had I seen such marvels of engineering. In the same way the top spiraled upward, so too did the interior spin down. Our path grew steadily taller and wider before opening to a grand chamber with yet another, somehow vaster city below.

Curiously, there seemed to be a second ocean atop it, though it held the shiny film of an air bubble.

I'd read of this phenomenon before; it was a place where two densities of water met but couldn't mix. Trish tried to take the submersible into it, but we "bounced" off the surface. It was too dense for our craft to penetrate.

I was content to take pictures for future evaluation, but whatever glistening film kept us from entering caused the pictures to blur—not just out of focus, but beyond recognition.

We traveled above the city like zeppelin through the clouds.

Curiously, it appeared creatures walked among the streets, beings of unusual make and limb assortment. Some might have been sentient plants, walking on rooty feet, while others had wings and the shine of chitin. There were masses of wholly writhing tentacles, slipping around corners. Others remained beyond the description of our pitiful language.

All of this in a city with non-Euclidean geometries, roads which seemed to stretch endlessly ended only a short time later. Buildings which rose and turned seemed to follow us, keeping the same face angled toward us regardless of perspective. At times the denizens appeared taller than the highest edifice, while occasionally they faded to little more than dots far below. It was impossible to gain any reasonable bearing without nausea burbling forth.

"Oh shit!" Trisha moaned. "Which way did we come from?"

Fear trickled down my spine as my stomach threatened to evacuate its contents. "You don't know? I thought you were keeping track."

We were so lost in the sights below that we'd veered off course. The city below seemed an endless maze without landmarks. With instruments going haywire, there was no way to determine from which way we'd come.

"Damn..." I muttered. "There has to be—"

I paused as a shockwave rippled through us, jarring me against her. If not for our restraints, we'd be piled up on the floor.

"What the hell was—" Trish was cut off by a cacophonous rumble, like a voracious trumpet or an endless, ever-growing gong.

Most sounds were dampened by water, but this reverberated steadily increasing in power until we both clutched our ears. The creatures below noticed it as well, pandemonium erupted in the streets as every kind of creature imaginable scattered.

Whispers skittered through my mind like many-legged bugs, a terrible, harsh language of spite and madness. Chanting, screaming, and the euphoric ululations of triumph.

Then a chorus of every language cried out in unison.

"The devourer is here! She lives again! T'sagothoxix, mother of hungers, comes for us all!"

I screamed and saw Trisha doing the same, but both were drowned in the insane dissonance.

Then, I looked through the glass and saw it. Lit by the innate glow of the city below, a nightmare crawled along the top of the cavern. Limbs jutted along its endless frame, mouths on stalks joined them, but the defining feature was a gaping, many-toothed maw. Clusters of what might be eggs lined its sinewy body like a pestilence, and before our eyes, they ruptured in a nuclear green cloud of ichor. Swarms of horrors swirled out and descended upon the city, falling upon the residents and rending them to tatters in moments. No two were alike aside from, like their progenitor, a wide, hateful mouth filled with fangs.

As if to punctuate our own fate, one of Trisha's lifeless whales lay tangled in the rows of teeth. One had gouged through its core. The scale was immeasurable; that singular immense prong made this whale, larger than a school bus, look like a bit of gristle.

Another horrid howl erupted from the beast, and Trisha, ever more competent than me, drove the control forward and held it.

Our little submarine rocketed forward only a few hundred feet when the flow of water around us reversed. The great, gaping blackness pulled us toward it and our doom.

The engines were no match for such fury, and I believed that we would be enveloped by the inky void. We crested the last of a hundred rows of razor, boulder-like teeth before another great exhalation sent us careening madly away.

Our vessel vibrated with incredible force until my bones threatened to shatter in place. My ears bled. My eyes bulged.

She held steady and moved at an angle away from the dreadful beast.

Screaming with a grin bordering maniacal, she pointed, and I saw it too. The tunnel from which we'd come. It was perhaps two hundred yards further.

Then, the mighty undertow drew us back once more, away from safety and the promise of freedom. It ripped all hope from our hearts.

As we spun, I saw the abomination closing on us. Whatever senses it used had managed to locate us, and trillions of legs and tentacles snatched the stone, propelling it forward.

The vacuum ended, and we again moved toward our only

escape.

It was dozens of feet behind us, darkness swirling within its jaws. I turned back and saw, to my confusion, an infinity of shining lights. It was like looking at the night sky on a cloudless night without another light for a thousand miles in any direction.

For all the world, its insides looked like space.

Then, the horror disappeared behind worked stone. Runes glowed across its surface in a rainbow of colors. We'd made it to the spiral!

She wove us through the tunnel, but from behind came a calamitous jarring hammer blow. The corridor around us shuddered, and hulking chunks of masonry crumbled away, falling all around our submersible.

My wife steered us away from the worst of it, but crumbs of stone clattered against its hull.

"We won't hold together if this keeps up! It'll tear us apart."

Her words made me realize the insanity in my brain had faded to a dull background noise. I laughed aloud at the relief of it.

It withered and died under her furious glare.

Not a moment too soon, we plunged back through the opening and into the ancient city. It too rumbled, tall spires crumbling down on itself.

She didn't waste time trying to escape it, instead opting to rise far too quickly. My ears buckled under the pressure, and I saw her own bleeding freely. But it didn't matter if we survived.

The radio crackled, but we could only hear a word here and there. "Tremors", "Christ!", "Goddamn seaquake," "out of there!"

Our lights grew brighter until sunlight turned it to jade, then green glass.

Trisha's eyes fluttered and I knew neither of us could keep this up for much longer.

The whispers suddenly returned, growing stronger, louder, and with my last conscious vision, I turned back to see the infinite maw below. It enveloped all else as it came for us.

Reaching for Trisha's hand, I just managed to grasp it before my sight faded to a crimson cloud.

I woke to her sobs. It must have been bad, as she never cried. She was too professional for tears.

It took a moment to gather my bearings, but when I did, I unfastened my restraints to join her huddled on the floor. Warning lights flashed, and a soft voice threatened, "Oxygen Levels Catastrophically low," over and over.

I wrapped myself around her, desperate to provide any

comfort. When she'd calmed enough, she answered my unasked question with a finger. It pointed out of our viewing port.

Looking beyond it, I saw to my dismay, not an ocean floor or crashing waves, but a planet with six rings. It looked like an atom from a distance, though the surface was a pale orange. Further, a starscape twinkled out forever.

"What the hell?" I gasped, feeling the lightheadedness that was a sure sign of oxygen deprivation.

Her sobs became cackles—wild, crazed sounds that froze my heart.

"It's space! Fucking space! We're in the goddamn void!" She gulped air, but continued half-laughing, half-crying.

Just as when we'd neared the ocean floor, curious creatures drifted by. Glowing, blinking things without reasonable shape or logical bodies. Some were clear, others were pale.

I couldn't help but consider how beautiful they were, even as my lungs burned. How incredibly lovely these lifeforms were. Part of me wondered if they'd come from the leviathan, or if it had swallowed them, too.

None of our equipment could quantify or properly evaluate the things we'd seen. Our species, our planet, our galaxy; none of it mattered. Nothing ever really had.

Bert Lestrange's works include various degrees of Horror, Fantasy, Weird Fiction, and, occasionally, unadulterated Smut. He is the husband of Marie Lestrange, world traveler, and self-proclaimed foodie—though he has a weakness for gast station chilli dogs. He and his family's roots spiderweb across the mountains of East Tennessee. Caregiver, father, and proud ally.

Nicest asshole you'll ever meet.

Lost At Seafood

L.W. Young

Entry 1

I have been lost for almost three days now. I fear I shall die out here.

To anyone listening to this, the research Nathaniel and I carried out aboard the Southern Explorer must not be left to perish at the bottom of the ocean. What we discovered could change this world forever.

Please, whoever you are, promise me that...

Entry 2

Somehow, my raft and I survived last night's storm. If there were anything out here, I wouldn't even be able to see it through the impenetrable white fog surrounding me. I'm weary from hunger, but not ready to die. The Southern Explorer may be gone, but its legacy must now live on through me.

Nathaniel would want me to carry on our life's work…

Entry 3

I can see something in the mist, although I'm not sure how to describe it…

It's an enormous black tusk rising out of the water. It appears sturdy, but it couldn't possibly be connected to the ocean floor all the way out here, could it?

Entry 4

I'm closer now. What the hell is this thing?

Entry 5

After circling the enormous tusk, I've discovered a hollow in its structure. I was even able to shore my dinghy inside. I'm going to explore the interior on foot…

Entry 6

The texture inside the tusk is unlike anything I've seen before. It's remarkably brittle, almost like charcoal, yet strangely organic looking. The only visual comparison that comes to my mind is the medical condition Fibrodysplasia ossificans progressive, otherwise known as petrified muscle…

Wait, someone's coming…

Entry 7

Okay, God, where do I even start?

After recording my last entry, I was set upon by a gang of

men who seemingly appeared out of nowhere from inside the tusk. I tried to fight back, but I was too weak. Inside their grip, I found myself being dragged up what felt like a flight of stairs in total darkness. I pleaded with them, but their babbling, gurgling replies held little trace of humanity.

Finally, I was thrown through some doors near what must have been the peak of the tusk structure and met with a blinding stream of daylight. With my arms and legs free, I sat up and looked around my strange new setting.

I was in a restaurant. A man-made restaurant.

And that wasn't even the strangest part...

"Welcome!" a voice said.

I turned to it and saw Charles Novelli. Yes, that Charles Novelli; celebrity chef, tv personality, youngest man ever to win four Michelin stars and the first to hand them all back, and whose wife was found brutally murdered three years ago before he went missing himself.

Picking me up again, the ones who dragged me here dumped me on a seat on the table opposite Charles. In the light of day, I finally got a look at these men. They looked more like beasts to me; their pale, anaemic complexions betrayed the rippling muscles and tight veins winding around their bodies. They were also all dressed in tight-fitting waiters' uniforms.

Meanwhile, sitting opposite me, Charles lowered his wine

glass and gave me a cold, slippery smile.

"Welcome to my kitchen." He bowed.

"I... is this a dream?" I asked, pushing away on my chair.

He just laughed, reaching across the table to lay his hand on mine.

"It's no dream, my dear," he smiled, "and I admire your determination for making it here."

"I... I wasn't looking for this place. My boat sank, you see, my husband and I were conducting important research..." I slipped my hand away, "W...where am I?"

"Where you're meant to be," he told me with a wink, "We all arrive here sooner or later."

With a brisk clap of his hands, Charles's white-clad servants erupted into motion. From the kitchen, I heard the clatter of pots and pans.

"Listen, I don't have time for this," I insisted, fighting for Charles's attention through crisscrossing arms as his subordinates lay cutlery out before me. "I must get home. Now!"

"And so, you shall," Charles sat perfectly still with his hands folded, "in fact, the necessary preparations are already being made."

"They are!" I leaned across the table, grabbing his collars. "How? When?"

"All in good time," Charles interrupted, gently withdrawing

my hands, "but first, you must agree to one condition."

"What condition is that?" I obliged, listening.

"You must be my guest for the evening."

"Your... guest?"

He nodded. I remained silent.

"You shall remain here and eat a special dish which I will freshly prepare for you," he elaborated, his eyes beaming at me. "After that, you may leave."

"I..."

"Do you accept my terms?" he shot the question across the table, drumming his fingers on the cloth. "Yes or no?"

"All I have to do is... eat your food?" I asked.

He answered with a simple wink.

I put on my most convincing smile and nodded. If I understood anything about this situation, it was that I couldn't die now. I needed to get my research back to the world, and if it took wining and dining with an accused murderer on his obscure hideout in the middle of uncharted waters, then I was willing.

Besides, I was also very hungry.

Charles stood up, and two glassy-eyed servants rushed to his sides. Swiftly, they fitted him with an apron, gloves, and placed a net over his wiry hair. With fierce-eyed intent, he stomped across the dining area towards the kitchen.

"Wiiiiiine, maaaaaadam?"

The drawl came from the vacant-eyed, pale-skinned zombie who stood next to me with a bottle in his hand.

"Please…" I coughed, squeezing my trembling limbs together tightly as he poured.

The stink of salt rising from the kitchen was almost overpowering. As the sizzle of oil, flame and garlic powder faded, one of the gaunt, pale-faced waiters came out carrying a plate with a slimy, black snake sitting on it. I tried not to wretch as he slammed the dish down in front of me.

"Please, have a taste." Charles emerged from the kitchen, dabbing his sweating forehead as he stalked back over to my table. "It won't bite, not anymore."

I prodded the quivering tentacle with the side of my fork. It's jelly-like texture was unlike any species I knew of.

"Eat up." Charles clapped excitedly, creeping closer. "It'll get cold."

Squeezing my eyes shut, I tore a chunk out of the inky black tentacle and shoved it into my mouth. Once the slippery flesh hit my tongue, everything was different.

My eyes bloomed and I chomped contentedly. This was the best food I'd ever tasted! However, not only did it nourish me within seconds, but I could feel my mind expanding too, suddenly gaining an affinity for memories and knowledge I couldn't possibly account for.

"What is this?" I exclaimed, unable to keep away from another mouthful. "This is Great!"

Charles tapped his nose in a knowing gesture.

"How did you come across such a species?" I leant across the table. "I just have to know!"

"I like your curiosity." He nodded with a nostalgic smile. "I wish my previous wife had shown such traits."

Soundlessly, I swallowed and tried not to let the sudden panic appear on my face. Crossing his legs, Charles nonchalantly turned his gaze to the window.

"She was a good woman, but she didn't truly believe," he mused, looking out over the sea. "So when my mission required a personal blood sacrifice, the choice was a little easier."

He swallowed the contents of the glass in several heavy gulps before wiping his lips and turning back to me, his eyes cold.

"S...sacrifice?" was all I could say.

"To awaken the Ancient One, of course," Charles said obviously.

I gulped dryly. Although I had no idea what he meant, the two words brought an onset of immense dread for reasons I couldn't quite explain.

"O...of course," I said, dabbing my mouth as I tried not to choke. "In fact, I... I'm quite familiar with the 'Ancient One' myself, you know?"

At this, Charles rolled his head back and let out a deep, booming belly laugh. I laughed along with him while cold sweat broke out all over my body, hoping this tactic of deception would pay off.

"Well, of course you are." he sat up, wiping a tear from his eye, "after all, you've been dining on him for the last ten minutes."

"What...?" I choked.

"Three years ago, my team discovered a petrified tendril standing above sea level in the Southern Pacific," Charles explained, shutting his eyes dreamingly. "I knew then that I'd performed the blood ritual correctly."

My skin went cold. So, he had killed his wife?

"The black tusk..." the words left my mouth.

Charles nodded.

"I suppose it would look like that to the uninformed viewer." He stared through me and laughed. "Don't fret, the beast still lies dormant below the ocean waves. I intentionally did not complete the awakening ritual, you see. It was never my intention to fully wake up the Ancient One."

"Then why do it?" I leant across the table, suddenly caring

deeply about the new developments in this horrific tabloid story. "What did you stand to gain?"

Charles offered a slippery grin. "To taste him," he said simply.

I shook my head, still not understanding.

"Taste him?"

"The Ancient One's flesh became brittle and solidified above sea level, perhaps due to my incomplete ritual." He nodded, smiling slyly. "However, the submerged part of the beast still maintains a succulent fleshy texture."

"So what?" I shook my head. "You forged a restaurant inside the solid part!?"

"Quite the perfect structural material, no? All I needed was to bring along some propane tanks, dry ingredients, and my faithful servants to apply the finishing touches to the decor," he chuckled, casting his eyes around the room. "As for the menu, the only way to preserve the beast's flesh for long term consumption before it petrifies out of water is by immediately cooking or freezing it. I didn't exactly have many location options, did I?"

He raised his wine glass to his mouth. I put my cloth to my lips, trying not to be sick.

"Then how do you..." I swallowed my nerves. "How do you harvest it?"

"My crew, enhanced by the power of the beast's own cooked flesh, carry out diving missions to restock my supply," he told me, casting a glance to the pale-faced men waiting around our table. "They're very loyal."

"They…" I trembled, casting worried glances at them. "They can do that?"

"They are very loyal," he elaborated simply, "and excellent swimmers."

It was then that I noticed the waiters hungrily regarding the empty black smears on my plate as if ready to pick it up and start licking it clean right in front of me.

"What about you?" I asked. "Aren't you worried about how dangerous this might all be?"

To this, he rolled his eyes.

"My goal as a chef has always been to discover the ultimate flavour, whatever that entails." He motioned to my empty plate. "I'd say I've found it, wouldn't you?"

With that, he departed, telling me that my means of travel would be ready in the morning. I'm in a guest room inside the solid part of the tusk now, still thinking about the words Charles left me with. Honestly, I'm a little offended by his comparison towards my own ambitions with his sick experiments of summoning ancient occult Gods just to enable a pretentious dining experience.

Actually, that's a lie.

I'm also thinking about how amazing that meal was…

Entry 8

I can't believe I'm going to die like this…

I was awakened in the middle of the night by a voice whispering from the darkness.

"Whose there?" I hissed.

"They're coming…" the floaty voice responded, seeming to approach me from all directions. "Get out…"

I didn't recognise the voice, but there was a quality to it that seemed strangely familiar. I went to my door, opening it a crack, and heard the low hush of Charles ordering something to his henchmen.

The beast men started coming up the stairs. Using the cover of darkness, I dashed up the central staircase ahead of them. However, as their flickering lanterns got closer, I realised that there was nothing to hide behind. Holding my breath, I pulled in my tummy and flattened myself against the nearest wall, hoping to blend into the shadows. The glassy-eyed henchmen either didn't see me or were too dumb to deviate from their orders, because they kicked down my door and burst in without even looking ahead of them. While they were pulling my room apart, I slipped down the staircase they had just come up.

But then, just as the sparkling moonlight from the hollow alcove became visible, my stomach growled. My mouth started to salivate as my tongue tingled. I didn't want to leave this place yet, I just had to taste it again.

Then, the floaty voice which I'd heard inside my room came back to me.

"There'll be chances for that later…" it told me, whispering inside my head. "Remember your promise to Nathaniel…"

Whatever this voice was, I felt I could trust it. I raced down the staircase and emerged into the alcove, seeing the mouth of the cave opening out onto the dark ocean. My rescue dinghy was tethered before it, bobbing on the waves like a lapping tongue.

But standing with his boot on the inflated rubber was Charles Novelli. He stared at me, amused.

"Leaving, so soon?" He crossed his arms and leant forward.

"We had a deal," I told him, jabbing my finger. "You said you'd take me home!"

"I did." He shrugged, checking his nails. "This place is your home now."

I stood my ground. Leaning off the boat, he strutted over to me.

"Don't you want to stay here under our care?" he asked.

"Our?"

"My servants would love to have a female amongst their ranks," he snarled. "They've only had each other's company for so long."

"Are you out of your mind?"

Looking back on it, it was a pretty redundant question. He reached out to me.

"Come now, it's not like it'd be a one-sided deal." He laughed, laying a delicate hand on my cheek. "I'd cook for you every night, just as I do for my other servants."

That's when I heard the voice whispering in my ear again...

"Strike him..." the voice hissed, lusting for blood. "NOW!"

While Charles's wrist was by my face, I turned my head and bit down on it. Part of me feels like whatever presence was whispering inside my brain had endowed me with enhanced strength, because my teeth ripped through his tendon like paper. As black blood sprayed out and coated me, he stood staring at his mangled hand in fascination and disbelief. That's when I shoved him over, hearing a satisfying crack as he landed on the crusty flooring.

After I'd stamped over to my boat and uncoiled the rope, he grabbed my leg. I went to the floor, reaching out for my floating dinghy as it came loose from the tether and started to float away. Rolling over on the brittle ground, I raised my boot before landing it on Charlie's head. Breaking into a run, I dived into the escaping dinghy and landed inside face first.

But as I was peddling away, I felt something dragging me down. Charles was still clinging to the dinghy's netting, fighting to get onboard.

"You'd really turn your back on my incredible food?" he screamed over the splashing water as he kicked and struggled to get onboard. "You'd turn your back on paradise!?"

But then, the struggling stopped.

"Charles?" I asked, panting.

Nothing.

I looked overboard and saw nothing but faint ripples on the surface of the moonlit water. Something beneath the waves must have grabbed him and pulled him down.

Thinking about it now, I wonder if perhaps the blood from Charles's wrist had awoken the 'Ancient One' just enough to help itself to a little snack before it returned to hibernation...

Maybe one day I'll get to come back and study what's really down there...

Entry 9

I'm lying on my back in the raft, exhausted from paddling to get away from that place.

After staring into the moonlit dark for hours, I finally realised that I'm lost again, this one last flare is the only hope I've got left. I feel the enhancements bestowed by the tentacle starting to fade now, but I can still hear that singular voice in my head telling me not to lose hope, not to give up...

I wonder if anyone will find me.

Entry 10

I can hear the horn of a cargo ship, thank GOD!

Entry 11

I made it back to civilization.

I told people about what happened, but no trace of the black tusk structure was ever found out there in the ocean.

During the whole ordeal, I'd also been pregnant with Nathaniel's baby.

The doctors tell me it should have died, but something kept it alive. They say it's a miracle....

I'm still trying to hold onto the idea that my conviction allowed our baby to survive. I had to deliver the Southern Explorer's findings on marine habitat migration to aid humanity's fight against climate change. That's what kept me going. That's what kept him going.

But even now, I still hear our baby talking to me in that same, floaty voice it had used while helping me escape Novelli's island.

"Everything will be okay..." it says. "One day, I will complete the ritual and the Ancient One will reawaken. Then, he'll take care of everything..."

He says that, if I do well, I might even get a chance to taste the delicious flesh of our Master once again before he uses me as his blood sacrifice to complete the reawakening ritual.

Apparently, it tasted good to him too...

L.W. Young graduated from the University of Kent with a BA Honors degree in English literature and creative writing. He has experience with writing for theater, film and YouTube, and is a passionate advocate of mindfulness and raising awareness of mental health issues. His favourite authors and influences include an eclectic bag: ranging from Stephen King to Cormac McCarthy to Ray chandler to David Mitchell to Kazuyo Ishigoda to Margaret Atwood and Colson Whitehead. However, if you ask him, he would probably tell you his favourite books are the Point Horror novels he read in his High School library as a teenager.

Sinister Waters

Bill Freas

Stoic Bay was a quiet enclave nestled away in a corner of a lesser-traveled beach of coastal Maine. Locals stayed away, but outsiders who knew of this quiet spot slipped in once or twice a summer to run their speedboats for a few hours on these tranquil waters that opened up into the Atlantic.

It was the evening of June 12, 2012. The sun began to set peacefully along a golden horizon. Its glow cast a striking reflection across the beautiful bay. James and Meg, a troubled married couple in their early thirties, strolled together down a trail, toward a dock. James soon got a bit ahead of his wife.

"James, wait. I can't walk that fast right now," Meg said.

He stopped and turned to her with a sigh. "Sorry…"

"Y'know, just go ahead without me. I don't think I want to do this."

"I thought we agreed this was a good idea for us right

now," he retorted.

She stood and looked away sullenly before her husband stepped forward and gently put his hand on her abdomen.

"It's not your fault. It's not anybody's fault. I told you – We'll try again soon. But tonight, we need to relax and clear our heads," he said.

She replied, "I don't deserve to have fun."

He took her in his arms and held her softly.

"You're going to be a great mom."

Their intimate moment was then interrupted by a grating voice from over at the dock. "Yo! How 'bout you two get a room first before you hop on my boat and make a mess, huh?!"

Meg and James peered over at the dock, where their obnoxious friend Ephraim and his bubbly, young girlfriend, Zenny, prepared his fancy speedboat, for a sunset bay run.

Zenny scolded Ephraim. "Leave them alone, you jerk."

"What? I have to establish some social ground rules here, babe. Or else, it'll be sheer anarchy on my beloved water craft," Ephraim replied.

James and Meg grinned and continued conversing quietly.

"Ephraim behind the wheel and in control of something that floats on water. Still a good idea?" she asked.

"Who else is going to listen to him brag about his big

promotion?" James asked.

The two chuckled lightly before James picked up his trek toward the dock. Before Meg joined him, a static shock pulsed down her back. She let out a small yelp of surprise as her hair stuck up a little from the unusual charge. Taken aback, she touched her hair and felt her skin, with curiosity, before catching up to her husband.

With a cigar fixed firmly in his cocky smirk, Ephraim stood behind the wheel of his high-end speedboat, driving Zenny, James, and Meg smoothly and swiftly through the bay, which they seemed to have all to themselves right now.

"Hey, uh, shouldn't we wear life jackets or something?" James questioned.

Ephraim took his cigar out of his mouth to talk. "What? Why?"

"In case your crazy ass wrecks this boat and sends us flying out into a watery grave."

Ephraim added, "Eh, life jackets are for pussies. Have some faith in your captain, James."

James peered at Meg, who rolled her eyes. Zenny maneuvered over toward the helm and wrapped her arms around her boyfriend.

"Aye, aye, Captain! Woo-hoo!" Zenny shouted.

Ephraim put the engine in a higher gear and took some

wild laps around the perimeter of the large bay and then out to the foot of the ocean. It wasn't long before the sunset, and the royal blue blanket of twilight took over. With the engine turned off, the boat floated calmly at the edge of the bay. The friendly foursome sat in a circle, drinking beer and enjoying some conversation in the peaceful environment.

"So, she pulled the tire iron away from me... Well, she grabbed it. She slapped my hand, really..." Ephraim said before turning to Zenny. "Y'know, you tell the story better."

"She slapped your hand and then your ass," Zenny said.

"She spanked my ass. In the middle of Home Depot. Like a goddamn second-grader. Mind you, I was wearing a suit. My best Armani."

James snickered and shook his head while Meg simply listened with a polite and distracted smirk.

Zenny asked her boyfriend, "Was that when she told you that she was going to use the tire iron to issue you a violent rectal exam?"

"Dammit, Zenny. You just gave away the funniest part. Go back to the part with the broken shopping cart."

James covered his mouth and cackled.

"Whoops. I forgot about that. I guess I screwed it up again," Zenny said.

"You people are loco supremo, man," James added.

Ephraim noticed that Meg was quiet and distant. "What's the matter, Meg? Coyote got your tongue?"

Meg snapped out of it and glanced at him as James sat up straight and cleared his throat. Zenny attempted to keep things light before Ephraim had a chance to sour the mood.

"This ocean air tires me out, too," Zenny said.

Ephraim continued, "Lots of coyotes out here around ol' Stoic Bay. In fact, coyotes were sacrificed and offered up to the great water spirits when the Wabanaki Indians buried their dead, here in this very bay."

"Enough jokes for one day, Ephraim," Meg replied.

"Who said I was joking?" he asked.

James spoke up. "C'mon, man, seriously. Let's not start with the scary stories. It's been a long week."

Meg's attention was abruptly drawn to the sky, where she witnessed a flash of bright, blue light.

"Did you just see that?" she asked.

"See what, babe?" James inquired.

"It was, like, blue lightning."

"Seriously?" Zenny asked.

They all looked upward, but nothing was there.

"Blue lightning? You sure it wasn't just some of James' Pabst Blue Ribbon doing the looking for you?" Ephraim scoffed.

"I haven't had any tonight," Meg retorted.

To their surprise, a very strange and abnormal rumble of thunder echoed across the shadowy landscape.

"Was that thunder?" Zenny inquired.

Ephraim replied, "I don't know, sugar. The sky looks pretty clear to me. Might have been a truck rolling along on the parkway."

"A truck on the parkway? You mean the parkway that's six miles away from here?" James questioned.

Ephraim was at a loss for words, and the mood quickly grew uneasy.

He began his response, "Look, all I know..." before everything was sharply overwhelmed by a raucous blast of the same bizarre thunder sound and a flash of blue light. Lying face down on the dock and completely soaking wet, Meg snapped out of unconsciousness by coughing a large volume of water from out of her lungs. Time had mysteriously jumped ahead, and it was now night. She rolled over onto her back and looked up at the black sky, with fear and confusion. An electrical whining and static sound filled the air around her. She closed her eyes and groaned with trepidation, fearful of how she got here and what happened.

Abruptly, she was back on the boat, with her husband and friends, just like before. The astonished woman found herself sitting safely in her same spot, even though she seemed to feel aware of the time slip that just occurred. James, Ephraim, and Zenny stood together and gazed down curiously over the side of the boat, where a large spotlight seemed to hover closely yet well beneath the surface of the water.

"Some of these models come with a spotlight under the boat. Zen, you wanna grab me the operating manual from out of the side compartment?" Ephraim asked.

James interjected, "This ain't a reflection from a light on the boat, Ephraim. That thing there is a self-luminous body."

"English, James," Ephraim replied.

"Whatever that is down there is casting its own light up at us."

"How would you know that?"

"You do remember when I got those two degrees in physics, right? The ones where I learned about science? Uh, I kind of know a lot about this stuff," James answered before Ephraim mocked him with a condescending jackoff hand gesture. "And this light has been following us across the lake for the last twenty minutes, growing brighter every meter or so," he continued. "How deep is this right here?"

"Right here? I don't know. Maybe two hundred feet in this spot. We're basically at the threshold of the ocean," Ephraim answered.

Zenny spoke up, "Guys, this is really starting to freak me out. I wanna go back to shore." Ephraim put his arm around her consolingly.

"Meg, you should see this," James said.

Still reeling from the uncanny metaphysical transition she experienced, Meg peered over at James.

"Hon, do you hear me?" James asked.

Suddenly, the light faded away.

"Look, it's gone!" Zenny exclaimed.

They all stared intently, but the illumination had now completely disappeared under the water.

"What the hell?" James said.

Shrill feedback and scratchy static resonated around them, causing them to hold their heads and cover their ears due to the intense physiological interference. To their absolute shock, choppy radio voices that sounded similar to their own voices began an intimidating interaction with them out of the disturbing air of their eerie atmosphere.

"Are you prepared to die tonight?" a radio-like, imitating voice of Meg questioned.

James peered at his wife with confusion. "Why would you say something like that right now?"

"I didn't say anything, James," Meg replied.

"The light shall return and drag you into a watery abyss of pain and torment," a radio-like, imitating voice of James called out.

"Stop saying those things! Stop it!" Zenny shouted.

Ephraim held his panicking girlfriend tightly. "What the fuck is wrong with you two?! Knock it off!"

"Does it look like our mouths are moving, Ephraim?!" James rebutted.

A radio-like, imitating voice of Zenny then broke through. "Soon, your warped minds and torn bodies will belong to us and to us alone." The frightening paradox of inexplicably hearing her own voice surround her sent Zenny into a full breakdown. She pulled away from Ephraim and hurried to the other side of the vessel.

"Zenny!" Ephraim hollered.

Unable to calm down, Zenny slipped and fell over the edge of the boat and into the water.

"Baby, no! Zenny!" Ephraim cried out.

Once again, a raucous blast of the same bizarre thunder and a flash of blue light ended the moment sharply, and Meg found herself back on the dock later in the night. Still soaking wet and lying on her back, she cried loudly. Things had somehow gone very wrong. Finally, she sat up and gauged her dark surroundings. The boat and the others were nowhere in sight. Desperately, she screamed out at the top of her lungs, "Help us!"

To her astonishment, a body floated face down on the water's surface, toward her at the dock. Without hesitation, she rushed over and tugged the distressed female body onto the shore, soon discovering that it was Zenny. The dead woman's entire face had been shredded and mauled, and her lifeless body was severely beaten and bruised. The sight of it all sent Meg into a terrified frenzy. The feedback and static filled the atmosphere once again before she tossed the body aside and prepared to run.

Suddenly, Meg was back on the boat, in her previous seat. James and Ephraim were both leaning over the side of the vessel, searching for the jettisoned Zenny.

"I don't see her! I can't see anything down there!" James said.

"Look harder! Reach down! She's got to be here somewhere! Shit! Zenny! Reach out for us, baby!" Ephraim shouted.

With tears streaming down her face, Meg spoke up softly and somberly. "She's gone... We all are."

The two men turned and stared at her.

"Fuck you, bitch. My girl ain't gone. We're not leaving here until she's back on this boat. So, help us find her, or shut the hell up," Ephraim replied.

Suddenly, the vessel was jarred by some impact from directly below it underwater.

"What was that?" James asked.

Ephraim answered, "It's Zenny!"

"That was not Zenny."

To their surprise, the boat was jarred again, only harder this time. They stood pat for a tense moment before being rocked by an even-more powerful jolt of impact. This last one was forceful enough to knock them around the vessel. Another hard hit supernaturally jolted Meg back to the dock, where she found herself kneeling and rocking back and forth on the cool, damp planks. She closed her eyes tightly and covered her ears, engulfed with mental anguish.

The radio-like voice that mimicked her before whispered hauntingly in her head. "Open them... Open them." She heeded the command, taking her hands off her ears and whipping her eyes open, not knowing what she would see or hear next.

Ominous silence set in while she gazed out onto the shadowy bay. After a few moments, the boat drifted by right in front of her at the end of the dock. James and Ephraim were both onboard. Their bodies were covered in lacerations, and their faces were shredded like Zenny's. Meg shivered and wept before bursting into a fit of hysterics. Shifting to survival mode, she rose to her feet shakily and turned around to escape. To her absolute horror, a malevolent alien invader stood on the other end of the dock. This tall, cloaked being was a ghastly, black silhouette accompanied by a menacing, fast-strobing light that radiated behind and around it. The woman stood frozen with terror and watched the foreign creature as it moved its long arms and let out some blood-curdling, inhuman screeches. In one last attempt to escape the nightmare, Meg turned and sprinted to the edge of the dock. With one big leap, she launched off the boards and plummeted into the cold, murky water.

Astoundingly, Meg found herself back at the beginning of it all. She and James were walking toward the dock to meet up with Ephraim and Zenny at their boat, as before.

James stopped and turned to Meg with a sigh. "Sorry..."

With wide eyes, Meg tried to assess her latest reality.

"What the hell is happening here, James? Please, help me..."

"I thought we agreed this was a good idea for us right now."

She looked at him very anxiously before he stepped forward and gently put his hand on her abdomen.

"It's not your fault," he said. "It's not anybody's fault. I told you—we'll try again soon. But tonight, we need to relax and clear our heads."

Tears filled up in her eyes, worry boiling in her gut.

"We need to get out of here, James. Right now."

"Shhh... It's alright, Meg. Everything's okay. I got you," he replied.

"We have to go. Before it's too late. I can't control this. They hide down in the ocean, but they prey on the bay. They prey on this bay and anyone who goes near it."

James was perplexed. "Prey on the bay? Meg, what are you talking about?"

Their intimate moment was then interrupted by a grating voice from over at the dock. "Yo! How 'bout you two get a room first before you hop on my boat and make a mess, huh?!"

The two looked over at the dock, where Ephraim and Zenny once again prepared his fancy speedboat, for the evening bay run.

Zenny scolded Ephraim. "Leave them alone, you jerk."

"What? I have to establish some social ground rules here, babe. Or else, it'll be sheer anarchy on my beloved water craft," Ephraim replied.

Meg pushed away from James and broke down completely.

"No! No! I won't go out there! I won't do it! We have to leave! Please! Please! Help me!... Help me!" she yelled.

Studying under esteemed writers Sonny Sykes and Charles McClelland, Bill Freas continued his education at West Chester University before he was hired in 2002 as the head writer of a TBS sketch-comedy pilot that ultimately did not make it to series. Subsequently, he optioned or sold over two dozen scripts, which included shorts, features, and pilots. As an author, he has written more than twenty published short stories, including three full collections. His produced credits as a writer span multiple genres and mediums. Currently, Bill also heads up Oceanicom Films' development department, where he oversees the development of US and international film and TV projects for the Australian company. Along with script, development, and production consultation, Bill is also a staff writer for Vancouver production company Foresight Entertainment, with which he has had an active partnership for over fifteen years.

Carmen San Diego Underwater Cruise

Cody Matthews

It is 12:00 pm November 11, 2011. I'm Anna Madison. I've been hearing whispers all day, something I never got used to, but I tried to ignore them.

I sat in my dark, blue-walled kitchen with the red curtains open, the light outside illuminating the room. Reading an article about the all-women cruise in celebration of the 1920's women's rights victories.

But my main suspicion about going on this cruise is the story about the 100-year-old woman, Carmen Ray, who was a model in 1947 that started a magazine to empower women, which became a sensation after her second issue, Ray: Everyone's A Star. Inspiring thousands of young women to pursue bigger careers like producer and electric engineer, eventually becoming a producer herself, producing and writing the underground film, "Salon Dream." At this time, her and julio were dating, julio being a real estate worker with his own neighborhood, Julio Ray Drive. But to celebrate her success, they both decided to take a cruise across the pacific ocean. Julio paying his friends to help him paint her name on the side of the cruise, so the cruise would draw more attention– given how known she was. But.. Shot herself on the cruise after Julio killed a couple people before shooting himself. They say his victims were mutilated, and a cut-up arm was found with a black tooth in it. There was a note on Julio's body, saying he didn't want his wife to figure out his plans to kill her. What "last plan?"

Julio was the only male passenger that Veronica Mince, the cruise's captain, accepted on the ship. Something I found odd, and the fact that this happened on the underwater cruise I was about to go on scared me. It made me weary about even going. I slid my finger down the Macbook touchpad, coming across a black and white photo of Julio Ray.

Something about his picture creeped me out. In the picture, he had thinning, greasy gray hair, and was wearing a tux. A wrinkly face, with no eyelids or lip line. I could also see a dark oil-like stain on the bottom of his mouth.

I wasn't sure if I wanted to go on this cruise anymore. It was creeping me out, almost as much as the whispers traveling through the house were.

Feeling a cold breeze behind me, I turned around to see Elliot and Amy standing side by side, holding the Kewpie dolls to their chests. Both of them wearing what the dolls were wearing: Amy with a white dress and black button shoes, and Elliot with a black blazer, black pants and loafers. They never left the house, always stood next to each other, and never played. They sat on Elliot's bed all day, staring at the wall.

They just stood there, their faces pale.

"Yes, sweethearts?"

"Why are you leaving?" Elliot asked in a flat tone, a subtle whisper behind it.

"We're going on vacation. Are you guys packed?"

"We're happy here, mommy," Amy said with a cold smile.

I tried to ignore the feelings I got from them. I wanted to be happy, to believe I had a family, and to not feel like sobbing every day. But I had my kiddos, so why was I struggling with this? Was I afraid of losing them?

A couple of minutes later, I was packing the suitcases in the car, and a weird sting pierced my stomach. My chest felt heavy.

As we drove out of our neighborhood, we passed The Dean's Cemetery, passing a gravestone with dozens of flowers around it, which my eyes fixated on:

AMY MADISON, 08-28-03 to 11-11-06. DEATH: CANCER. REST IN PEACE, SWEETHEART.

Is that a coincidence? She's in the back seat with Elliot. She's been alive for over a year now...

I turned back to the road, driving in the wrong lane, a car approaching me. I jerked the wheel to the right, screeching out of the way, hearing thousands of people whispering in the back seat. I glanced in my rearview mirror, seeing Amy and Elliot as cool as cucumbers. Both of them with lethargic faces and dark circles around their eyes. Holding their kewpie dolls close to their chests.

I tried to give them a warm smile. Nothing.

1 PM. I'm at the cruise port, ready to board the ship. I couldn't believe how big and long this ship was. The port was filled with women. I decided to wear the same white dress Amy was wearing, trying to start a conversation with her about girly things, but she and Elliot stood there with their dolls to their chests the whole time, saying nothing.

The ship was a slick-looking white with a pink heart design on the side, and black text, "Carmen Ray's Underwater Cruise." Standing on the long wooden port, I saw hundreds of people in line, some of them dressed up, and some in Hawaiian dress shirts. Before I knew it, we were in a fancy room in the underwater suite, deep underwater, and too late to turn back. Because the second we stepped into the room, I felt sick.

9 PM. Elliot and Amy just sat on the edge of the left side bed, staring at the wall. The crystal chandelier lights kept flickering,

and the whispering got worse. The room had beautiful gold and red carpeting, white wallpaper with roses printed on it, and closed tan curtains. But I couldn't focus on any of that because of the denseness in the room. I felt like I had a high fever, my body feeling pushed in and heavy at the same time. We stayed in the room for what felt like years—finally, I left to get some food, though my appetite was non-existent.

The hallway leading to the lobby door was dark. The red and gold carpeting was creepy-looking in the dim light, but—why was it so quiet?

I made my way down the dark hallway, encountering framed pictures of Carmen Ray, the 100-year-old lady I had been reading about back at the house, her husband's pictures further down, slit marks in both of their throats, something I thought was just an artistic mistake, assuming the pictures were painted.

Zzzzz! Zzzzz! The alarms pierced the dense silence, the nerves in my head ringing with each buzz, the hallway floor feeling like an elevator descending to its destination. The alarm sound was flaring louder, and LOUDER.

All I could think about was Amy and Elliot—I need to get back to them! I need to get back home to see if they're okay— wait, they're here! Where am I? The whole ship made a big thud noise and shook. I started running back down to the room for Elliot and Amy, when I froze in the middle of the hall, blacked out. But I was somewhat conscious.

"He's gone! He's gone!" I screamed and wept.

I came back to, thinking I'd just fallen asleep.

I couldn't open the door. It somehow got stuck, or maybe I locked it. So I broke it in with my shoulder. At this point, I had a strange, dissociated feeling, like I wasn't living my own life anymore, going in and out of consciousness. Speaking was getting harder,

"Eliii! Aii!" I couldn't say their names. I wanted to say someone else.

"We're–we're–we're dead, mommy!" Echoing in my ears, struggling to find where they were. They weren't sitting on the bed anymore. The room, dark and freezing. The curtains were open, a distant light from the bottom of the Pacific Ocean barely lighting the room. Turning to each side of the room, then entering the bathroom, running out of the bathroom to check the left bed.

Nothing. Nothing but the Kewpie dolls with ink-void eyes, and for some reason, as I glanced at the Kewpie dolls, I felt something coming, something that wasn't coming fast, but wasn't slowing down.

The simple task of blinking was sickening, each time, seeing what felt like me coming up the elevator, except I felt the same way as I felt in the hallway, like I was lifeless.

The elevator door opened.

That less than a second felt like a whole day. My eyes were slowly burning as I tried to keep my eyes open, yet I still knew something was even closer now.

"Aim–" I was interrupted by a raspy cough, "Amy!" I coughed again, "Elliot!"

My eyes were burning with tears. I needed to blink, but knew I'd see this thing again. The light under the entrance door didn't actually get brighter, but it forced my attention from my peripheral vision. The cruise had sunk. Why does it look brighter? The room temperature plummeted, my skin hurt, and my muscles trembled.

My eyes caved into the burning sensation, but this time I saw a woman. A woman with part of her face limp, her eyelid covering the limp eye, and the other side with a bulging eye, the iris a white cloudy color, eerily focused on what's in front of her. Her neck was cut open, blood surging down her white dress, her bony, bruised arms shaking, her fingers and legs dripping with blood.

Amy stands on the left side of her, and Elliot on the right, both having a pale blue-ish look, still wearing the same outfits. Amy and Elliot turn to the old woman, the woman's bulging, cloudy eye widens, slamming into the door with her shoulder.

POW, CRACK!! POW, CRACK! And just like that, my eyes opened. I couldn't stop coughing, my chest feeling heavier, and the room feeling colder. I tried to keep my eyes open as long as possible this time. And as the door cracked with every hit, I could feel the strength from the thuds, the weight going into the door. How is someone as old as her hitting the door with that much force? And what's happening to my Amy and Elliot? I take slow steps back,

"A–" I coughed uncontrollably, covering my mouth with my hands, then taking them away to find spots of blood.

The door broke open. Amy and Elliot stood there looking as if they were gonna be sick, but the old lady was nowhere to be found. I'm in tears approaching them. *Why are they acting like this?* I got closer,

"We're– we're– we're dead, mommy," echoed down the hall. I sobbed with my hands pressed to my chest,

"What the hell? What the hell!! I loved you! I know you're back! I'm not gonna feel like this!"

I kicked the chair in front of me, and knocked the picture frames off the wall. Then I dug my fingers into my hair, pulling strands out of my head. With the strands of hair in my hands I looked up, walking towards Elliot and Amy's bodies. The room had a greenish tint.

"Come on; we can go home." My voice broke. "We can go back to the way things were."

I turned to Amy. "I'll buy you that new china tea set you've been wanting—what do you say?"

I then turned to Elliot. "I can homeschool you if you want; do you want that?"

They stood in the entrance, maggots crawling down their hands and fingers, and blood seeping from their mouths. They're my babies. I'm just mentally ill and need to take better care of them. Elliot's and Amy's eyes tilted to my right. I turned around to the old woman, the left side of her head gaping open, only small strands of hair on the right side. The green tint made her look inhuman.

I grabbed the kids' hands, racing down the hallway, pushing the door at the end into the lobby and dining area, faced with mutilated female bodies littering the floor, forks stuck in two of the bodies. The floor was also covered in red carpeting and gold-like flower designs. Two chandeliers in front of me, one in front of the other. Shattered.

I made my way across the room, hearing a noise that I swore was a survivor. I sprinted to the bathroom area. It sounded like it was coming from there, and as I approached the bathrooms, a dangling fluorescent light flickered, the only light illuminating the lobby and dining area.

Entering the men's restroom, then the women's... Nothing. I opened the storage closet, grabbed three floatation life jackets and closed the door, taking a step forward—I froze in place.

"No! I love her! I won't eat her! I won't eat her!! Leave me alone!!!" The voice reverberated... POW!! A body hit the floor. I stood there, unable to move, and whoever that was, sounded like he was right beside me.

The moment I was able to turn around, a transparent old man with an oil-like stain on the bottom of his mouth, no lip line, no eyelids, visible black teeth, greasy short gray hair, bulging eyes, and a hole in his head. Forming a pool of blood on the floor around him. The guy looked to be 70 or 80 years old, but I recognized him.

I made a break out of the bathroom hall, and soon realized I wasn't holding my kids' hands. One of the last things I remember from the cruise before I was rescued a day later.

Next thing I knew, I was back in my kitchen, whispers still traveling through the house, but my kids were gone. They're not dead, though. They're still here with me. They're still my babies. And to this day, I wish I never took that vacation. I wish I could take it all back.

I'm Cody Matthews! I didn't always start with writing books, in fact, my dream was to become a script writer for mature cartoons on tv: like the simpsons and south park. A lot of my stories for these scripts I practiced writing were full of dark humor, whether if that was a younger sister killing people and stealing her mom's credit cards to go to a theme park; or if that was a mom character losing her mind, then starting a crappy comedy special on netflix. This is the stuff I wrote. It wasn't until later that my biological mom suggested writing books or short stories, something I didn't seriously consider, just because I was DEAD set on writing tv scripts. Granted, I had short stories in mind that I wanted to write. One of them was a magician that psychologically torments two siblings after they discover and open a dead magician's magic kit. Magicians still freak me out! Glad I'm not these kids! Anyways. Skip ahead. Several months ago, while prolifically posting on a FB horror story group, just seeing what kind of criticism I could get from my stories, and the next thing I knew, I was buying a book on amazon containing dozens of short stories by talented aspiring authors, including myself.

Human Voices Wake Us

J. Rocky Colavito

"Did you ever wonder if our presence here is disruptive to the ecosystem and its workings?" Melissa Gaynor asked her partner as they stared out the viewing port into the depths illuminated by the high-powered lights on the exterior of the Deep Water Platform.

Prentiss shrugged; if he were to be completely honest, he'd have answered, "Who gives a fuck?"

He was slowly going stir crazy from his current assignment: three miles deep on an exploration rig situated on an unstable sea bed, uncomfortably close to a slope that plunged deeper than their probes could handle. And that abyss was teeming with things that were better left alone. If the screen captures from the exploratory probes were accurate, whatever was down there had lots of teeth and unimaginable bite pressure.

"Probably," he answered, "but it doesn't matter to the people writing the checks, dissecting the samples, and using the data we collect. According to them, we're providing civilization with cutting-edge new knowledge that will positively affect future generations."

"That being said, what right do we have to exploit what's down here?" asked Gaynor. "I mean, the things we've discovered predate us by millions of years. They've claimed these lands and established a way of life. Who are we to invade and colonize that territory?"

Prentiss saw Gaynor as a cipher, an academic who was still too rooted in the life of the mind. Oh, she had all the right credentials, cross-disciplinary PhDs that straddled the arts and sciences, publications whose diction befuddled him, but which the other scientists in this rest stop on the way to hell ate up, and more time in undersea conditions than everyone else on the mission. But in the three months he had worked with her, he was still struggling to figure her out.

He suspected she was behind the disappearance of some valuable living samples of sea life that they had harvested, but he had no proof, and surveillance video yielded nothing substantial. Her complaints about exploitation were noted exceptions; the other members of the science crew nodded, recorded, filed, and forgot her recommendations—the scientific equivalent of saying "there, there" and patting her on the head. Prentiss was amazed that she didn't lash out at such treatment, writing it off as her knowing how the game was played and simply assuring that all objections were noted in the event of the shit going sideways.

"Gaynor, there's nothing wrong with what we're doing; we

are surveying, drilling cores, and harvesting samples of plant and sea life. We aren't polluting the ecosystem; our waste is stored and processed within the platform. What we are doing is no different than what goes on in the Amazon, Antarctica, in cave systems around the world. We explore, we look for answers, and we figure shit out."

"We weren't invited here, Prentiss; we are trespassers. And we're taking souvenirs. If you or I were to do such a thing at someone's house, it would be breaking and entering with theft."

Prentiss had heard this sermon many times since Gaynor had been dropped off as Harley's replacement. He conditionally missed Harley, a tattooed Amazon with few morals and fewer scruples. In spite of her wild attitude, she'd occasionally made Prentiss nervous, especially when it came to processing the specimens. It seemed that she'd enjoyed dissecting the living things a little too much; almost taking glee in the investigation of the inner workings.

One thing—Prentiss really had no name for it, and it defied description—that they'd collected seemed amphibious, and it gave off a loud squeak when Harley had split it from stem to stern with a scalpel. It struggled and tried to escape with its guts exposed, and Harley had pinned it to an examination tray with heavy-duty pins. It still struggled and squeaked pitifully until Harley figured out how to quiet it.

"Gaynor, I get it, you are the designated contrarian on this mission—"

She interrupted, "So that's why they made such a big deal out of my activist background?"

Prentiss sighed; more explanation meant more conversation, something he was already tired of.

"Yes, it's an old military concept; you have a group considering intelligence reports, findings, what have you, one person is the designated devil's advocate; whatever the group is for, they are against. The aim is to fully vet all possibilities. Your purpose is to remind us that there are consequences to our actions down here, and that the possibility of our doing damage may be greater than we suspect."

"Well, you all should feel that way." She said. She suddenly held up a hand to quiet the talking.

Prentiss squinted and saw it outside the viewing port.

It almost made him believe in mermaids.

It was mostly eel—no question there. The long, smooth body propelled it in an underwater ballet. The upper body revealed breasts and long, flowing tresses that resembled hair. The face had deep, probing eyes, and a human mouth that, when it smiled, revealed a serrated set of teeth that fit together seamlessly.

"She's beautiful," Gaynor said in awe as the creature pirouetted in the depths, claiming the light as if she were on stage.

"She's ours," Prentiss grunted as he started working the buttons to engage the capture system.

"Leave her alone!" Gaynor yelled as she grabbed at his hands.

Prentiss backhanded her; she stumbled backwards, holding one of her cheeks.

"Put hands on me again, and I will put you in the infirmary," he said. "You are a scientific advisor on this mission. What you just did is above your pay scale and borderline insubordinate. I could have you brigged for that. But I think you will have uses when we get this thing aboard." The system engaged, and Prentiss began sighting on the creature who was still dancing, seemingly enjoying itself.

The capture system that Prentiss operated was the underwater equivalent of a net gun; it fired a pulse that created a bubble around whatever specimen was being captured. The bubble solidified and was easily grasped by the "tentacles'—long cables that deployed and wrapped around the bubbles like a squid's appendages, drawing the bubble into the quarantine zone where whatever was captured would remain until it could be assured that it carried no dangerous elements to the platform's ecosystem. The company had learned from bitter past experience, losing two whole crews in its early years to a giant mollusk and a contaminant brought aboard by a salvage crew that mutated those it contacted into quivering masses.

Gaynor watched as Prentiss fired the weapon, and saw the creature encased in the bubble. It did not struggle against the confinement; it simply modified its dance into something that could work within the bubble. Gaynor watched as the tentacles extended and grabbed the imprisoned creature, pulling it forward into the isolation ward below.

Gaynor shuddered as the bubble passed the observation deck. She swore that the creature smiled at her before disappearing below.

Gaynor elbowed her way through the group of scientists—men and women—who were marveling at the creature freed from the capture bubble and released into a holding tank filled with water from the outside. The temperature was stabilized and the lights were dimmed so that it was not blinded by lights that it wasn't used to. Gaynor could see that the thing's eyes had already shrunk somewhat. They were nearly half the size that they'd been when she was captured.

Variously hued probe beams moved through the holding tank, and the creature swam lazily, occasionally floating upright and doing a fish's variation of a sexy shimmy.

"Hubba hubba," said one of the men, who was rewarded with an elbow to the ribs for his sexism.

The scientists collected their readings and went off to decipher them. One remained to deploy devices that would obtain a scraping and a fluid sample from the creature for analysis. She stilled her movement as the probes extended toward her, and stoically accepted the intrusions. Her skin where the scraping was taken immediately healed, a fact not lost on Gaynor or the technician.

"Did you see that?" he babbled in excitement.

Gaynor nodded; the creature swam toward the glass polymer

front of the tank and looked at Gaynor, who was entranced by the creature's eyes. There was knowledge within the specimen's gaze, even with a barrier separating them.

The creature bumped against the glass, pursed its lips, and planted a kiss where Gaynor's face hovered on the other side. It smiled the same toothy grin she'd observed when it was captured, and swam off, moving along like the eel it resembled.

Gaynor staggered backwards, holding her head, when the voice from nowhere announced its presence.

"Hello, human, we have much to discuss. In due time."

Gaynor collapsed; the technician hit the alarm.

"I think it talked to me," Gaynor said to the group of medical personnel that gave her a thorough and invasive examination when she'd been brought to sick bay. Multiple orifices ached from the insertion of various probes, one of which was still inside her vagina.

"Try to stay still, Gaynor; we're almost done here." The doctor was looking at the flashing readouts of Gaynor's body chemistry, and, she felt, spending a little too much time looking at where the last probe was still inserted.

Gaynor tried to relax and think of other things while the survey finished. The three beeps and the withdrawal of the probe signaled the conclusion. She waited to be told that she had imagined everything.

"Not a thing wrong with you that some deep, restful sleep won't help," the doctor said. "Everything codes as normal except for your stress indicators. I can guess the cause there. You really don't like what we're doing here, do you?"

"What do you think?" Gaynor flared at the older man.

"What I think is that you are a necessary part of this mission, and while you are doomed to frustration, you should realize that your input is valued."

"If it was valued, then why are we acting like we own this area, and can take what we want without thinking about the repercussions?"

The doctor sat back and glared at her. Gaynor was shocked by his sudden change.

"Dr. Gaynor," he said officiously, "the simple fact is that we—or to be more exact, the corporation—does own this area. It's bought and paid for, and all mineral and energy rights are ours to take. Ditto for anything that happens to inhabit it. The corporation is doing great work; if we can figure out what makes that new specimen self-healing, we could change the treatment of skin and tissue damage. The corporation is changing lives for the better." He took a breath. "Your objections are noted, but they are outweighed by the promise of human advancement. I am prescribing your immediate evacuation for further treatment that is not available here. You'll be headed topside in twenty-four hours, twelve of which will be spent in decompression. Until then, you are confined to quarters, where you will probably be collecting your belongings and readying yourself for evac." He stood and left her on the examination table.

Gaynor fumed as she pulled on her uniform. "This is what you get for doing your job", she raged. She heard the footsteps outside sick bay, and two security people, a man and a woman, stepped into view.

"I don't need an escort to my quarters; I know how to get around the platform," she sniped at the guards.

"We know that, ma'am," the woman said. "We're just here to make sure that you don't have any mishaps along the way."

Gaynor fumed as she stepped between the two guards and led the way to her quarters.

The guards stayed posted outside the door as Gaynor flopped on her lumpy bunk and stared at the ceiling one last time. What few possessions she had she didn't care much about, and so her packing took the time needed to stuff her laundry into a tote bag, slide her personal laptop into her backpack, and toss the few books and movies she'd brought to pass the time into the backpack's other compartments. That took an hour, and she still had eleven to be bored before she had to report for decompression.

"Hello again," said the voice.

Gaynor rolled off her bunk to thunk on the floor. She looked around the cabin.

"It's all in your mind, friend. We can have our conversation out of the hearing of your colleagues."

"You can hear my thoughts? You might not want to; I'm pretty pissed off at the moment."

"An easy emotion to understand, one that we have much experience with of late."

"What do you mean?"

"Melissa...can I call you that? I thought you of all people would understand. Your cautions that have fallen on deaf ears have been completely right. We are not happy with your kind for the intrusions, the gathering of our kind and environmental artifacts, and especially with the prying eyes you have dispatched into the abyss. There are things there that you cannot understand, and you have disturbed many of them, most of whom are less tolerant of your kind than I."

"Since you know my name, do you have one that I can use?"

"It resists translation into your language, so why don't you give me one?"

"Any preferences?"

"Something...what's your word, androgynous? I'm both male and female."

Gaynor thought for a minute. "How about Jules?"

"Why that name, out of curiosity?"

"Because there was an author who wrote a book about deep sea exploration. It was the most appropriate name I could come up with. It's commonly used as a shortened form of Julia, which was my mother's name."

"I appreciate it. Thank you."

"You're welcome. So, I'm right in saying that what we've done here has disturbed the ecosystem, and we've removed something that, down the line, is going to irretrievably mess things up down here."

The voice laughed. "Nothing so far-reaching; think of what you've done as the equivalent of poaching and trespassing. I've long made a study of your kind during your trips down here, and I've amassed a huge catalog of information from peeks into your various heads. I think something from one of your less-intelligent guards suffices in this situation. He has a sign in his quarters, it shows an act of bestiality perpetuated by something with antlers on a human, and it reads, 'Trespassers will be violated'; that is what is in store for you and your fellow humans."

"Any way I can be spared for sympathy to your cause?"

"I'm afraid not, but you will have it slightly better than the others here. You possess a quality not often seen in your kind—I believe you call it empathy. Our people find that intriguing, and hope to isolate the biological sources so that we might release them into the ocean. Our aim is positive pollution, with your kind consuming sea life that carries that trait. Maybe it will promote mutual respect for each other's spaces."

"Praiseworthy, but I don't think that goal is reachable."

"We have time; we've been down here for longer than your kind has inhabited the surface. We treated you as you do the inferior species. But you are persistent, and your encroachments have disturbed us."

Til human voices wake us... Gaynor thought.

"I'm not familiar with that."

"It's a poem that I like; there's lots of references to the sea and what lies within it. It's near the end."

"It fits; your kind's incessant chattering has annoyed us, and it is now time to—how do you say—shut you up?"

The voice took a harder edge, "Come, join me in the isolation section."

A loud siren indicating a structural breech shrilled. Gaynor looked out into the hallway as a large crack appeared, spraying water everywhere. Shouts and running feet echoed as safety protocols activated. Gaynor walked out of her cabin unimpeded, and was soon in the isolation section. She used her key card to let herself in and saw the creature—Jules—smiling at her as she entered.

"Join me in the tank; make haste. This area is going to breech in seconds."

Gaynor climbed to the top of the tank and opened the hatch used for feeding. The opening was just large enough for her to fit through. She took a deep breath and slid into the freezing water.

Jules swam to her and encircled Gaynor with her eel-like body.

The freezing temperature stabilized, and a protective bubble appeared around the two of them. Gaynor found that there was just enough air to allow her to breathe.

"Do not fear," Jules said as the side of the tank began to expand outward. "You will be safe with me. Your friends, I cannot promise the same. The old one is fierce, and while he will take specimens, he is also quite angry."

The side of the tank exploded outward, and the bubble containing the two of them blasted outward into the darkness. There was just enough light for Gaynor to glimpse what Jules had referred to as the old one. A huge creature, head like a prehistoric ammonite, with four arms and legs so long they were lost in the darkness below the edge of the sea shelf, was methodically dismantling the platform. Smaller beings, roughly human-sized, entered the station through cracks and emerged bearing the crew, struggling within bubbles.

Guess we'll find out what it means to be on the examination table; I hope Prentiss gets their equivalent of Harley, Gaynor thought as they left the light and dove deeper.

Hopefully, it's a place that will drown out the human voices.

After forty some years teaching at the college level and working in the different horror genres, Rocky is transitioning into horror writing full time. He is the creator of Buck Neighkyd, former porn star turned occult detective, the writer of The Extreme Giallo series, the spinner of Hardcore Splatter Wrestling Yarns, and the observer of The Nocutary Accounts.

Never Seen Again

Carietta Dorsch

"Police in Grenada report Ralph Hendry and Kathy Brandel, an American couple from Virginia, are missing after their boat was hijacked last week by three escaped prisoners," the radio news anchor announced from the living room.

"I wonder what happened," Sue said to her wife, Anna.

"I guess…" Anna paused. "I guess we'll never truly know. It's just sad."

One Week Ago

As the sun began to set over the calm waters of the sea, Ralph and Kathy sat on the deck of their yacht, sipping on glasses of champagne. The gentle breeze rustled through the sails, creating a soothing melody that filled the air. It was a perfect evening, a moment of peace and tranquility that the couple had been longing for after months of hard work and stress.

The sun was setting over the crystal clear waters of Grenada as Kathy and Ralph sat on the deck of their yacht, Simplicity, sipping on glasses of rum punch. The couple had been enjoying their winter cruising the Eastern Caribbean, exploring new islands and soaking up the warm sun.

As the sky turned shades of pink and orange, Kathy leaned back in her chair and let out a contented sigh.

"This is paradise," she said, raising her glass to Ralph.

Ralph smiled and clinked his glass against hers. "It sure is. I can't believe we get to live like this for a few months every year."

They had been sailing together for over a decade, ever since they retired and decided to fulfill their dream of traveling the world by sea. It had been a journey filled with adventure, laughter, and love.

But as the sun dipped below the horizon, a shadow seemed to fall over Kathy's face. Ralph noticed the change in her demeanor and reached out to take her hand.

"What's wrong, Kathy?" he asked, concern in his voice.

Kathy hesitated for a moment before speaking. "I've been thinking about our future, Ralph. We're not getting any younger, and I worry about what will happen when we can no longer sail."

Ralph squeezed her hand reassuringly. "We'll figure it out, Kathy. We always do. We can sell the yacht and settle down somewhere, maybe even start a new adventure on land."

Kathy nodded, but the worry still lingered in her eyes. She knew that their sailing days were numbered, and the thought of giving up their life at sea was a difficult one to bear.

As they sat in silence, watching the stars begin to twinkle in the night sky, Kathy felt a sense of unease settle over her. She knew that their time on the water was limited, and the uncertainty of what lay ahead weighed heavily on her heart.

But as Ralph wrapped his arm around her shoulders and pulled her close, she found comfort in his embrace. No matter what the future held, they would face it together, just as they had faced every challenge and triumph on their journey through life.

And as they sat under the stars, listening to the gentle lapping of the waves against the hull of their yacht, Kathy knew that as long as they had each other, they would always find a way to navigate the waters ahead.

Soon, they were both drifting off to sleep.

***

Thud

Thud

Thud. Thud. Thud.

Ralph and Kathy wake up suddenly from their top deck nap.
The stars twinkled with a foreboding glimmer like the gleam off a knife's edge.

"What was that?" Kathy asked in a whisper.

"Oh," Ralph said waving his hand, "probably just some waves, honey bunch. Want me to check it?"

"Nah," she said letting out a deep breath. "It's probably just waves. Let's just enjoy the stars."

Eventually they both went back to sleep.

***

Ralph and Kathy woke up to the gentle rocking of the boat as it swayed with the rhythm of the ocean waves. The sun was just beginning to peek through the clouds, casting a warm glow over the top deck of the boat.

Stretching and yawning, Ralph wrapped his arms around Kathy and pulled her close. She nestled into his chest, feeling the steady beat of his heart against her cheek as if they were recreating the scene from Dirty Dancing where Johnny showed Baby the rhythm to dancing was the same as a heart beat.

"I love you," he said with a gentle kiss to her forehead.

"I love you, too."

They had been sailing together for a few days now, exploring the crystal-clear waters the sea had to offer.

As they made their way below deck to start making breakfast, Ralph couldn't help but admire Kathy's beauty. Her short-cut, blonde hair seemed to glow in golden sunlight, and her eyes sparkled with that same mischievous twinkle that made him fall in love in the first place.

Together, they worked in perfect harmony, chopping mushrooms, cracking eggs, and brewing coffee as the smell of sizzling bacon filled the air.

Ralph shoved a piece of mushroom in Kathy mouth playfully, and she batted his hand away.

"Not before the omelet is done," she said with a smile as she picked up a piece of onion to shove at his mouth.

The small space was filled with much more laughter and love than one could ever imagine.

As they sat down to eat, Ralph reached across the table and took Kathy's hand in his. Their fingers intertwined, creating a bond that was unbreakable.

"I love you. You know that, don't you?" Ralph whispered, his eyes filled with a depth of emotion that spoke volumes more than words ever could.

"Of course I do, honey," Kathy replied, her voice soft and filled with tenderness. "How could I not? I love you, too."

Thud!

Thud!

Thud! Thud!

Kathy dropped her fork on her plate, "What was that?"

"Just waves honey," Ralph assured her, yet had an ominous feeling and couldn't quite place his finger on why.

Thud!

Thud!

Then a voice.

Then multiple voices.

Ralph grabbed his knife from his plate and motioned for Kathy to get behind him as he cautiously rose from his chair and made his way up the stairs. What they saw when they reached the deck made their blood run cold. There were two men, dressed in tattered prison uniforms, standing before them, their faces itched with desperation.

One of the men pointed a gun at Ralph and Kathy, his eyes filled with malice. "This is our boat now, bitches," he nearly gloated. "You two are coming with me."

"Follow him!" a man barked at them from behind. Making the total of men three.

Ralph startled, dropped the knife, and held on to Kathy.

"Let her go," one man demanded.

"No, keep them together," the tallest of the three said with a voice as smooth as Canadian rye whiskey. "We'll make him watch."

"Make me watch what?" Ralph hollered back as if he was not outnumbered.

"Oh you'll find out," he chuckled. "You'll find out.

***

Heavy breathing and muffled cries came from Ralph and Kathy as they struggled against their ties.

One of the men, a tall and burly figure, took pleasure in terrorizing Kathy, flicking her hair and thumping her nose with a cruel smirk on his face. Kathy whimpered, her eyes wide and brimming with tears as she tried to shrink away from his touch.

"Stop!" Ralph shouted.

"Stop this fuck head!" the man said as he brought the butt of his gun down out to Ralph's head with a solid blow.

Ralph let out a groan, spit shooting out of his mouth, and he cried out. "Fuck you!"

"Fuck me?" the man asked, bringing the gun down again.

Ralph slumped over unconscious, and blind to what was about to happen to Kathy.

***

The room seemed to close in on Ralph as his eyes adjusted to consciousness once again, the air thick with the sweat of the men and the coppery metallic scent of blood. Ralph looked down to see his beloved Kathy bruised and battered laying in a pool of her own blood. She was untied, but he knew she was too broken to even attempt moving.

"Fuck you! Fuck you!"

The man laughed, then pulled the trigger.

***

"The three men have been charged with capital murder in connection with the deaths of Ralph Hendry and Kathy Brandel. Trevon Robertson, 23; Atiba Stanislaus, 25; and Ron Mitchell, 30, were re-arrested on two counts of capitol murder," said the news anchor.

"Hey Anna!" Sue shouts. "They finally caught those guys."

"Well, at least we have that much closure."

Carietta Dorsch has loved horror movies since she was a little girl watching them at a way too earlier age and loves even more to share her love of horror with her writing. She also writes poetry, romance, and true crime.

When The Sun Goes Down

Devin Cabrera

"Drink up, boys! This is going to be one for the record books!" Kyle held his beer in the air.

His friends all cheered at once, holding up their beers as well.

Diego, their guide for the fishing trip, sipped his beer cautiously, looking out at the horizon. The sun was still pretty high in the sky, but was marching slowly toward the water below.

Just then, Kyle punched the boat forward, slamming on the controls, sending the boat rocketing through the water and creating a massive wake behind him.

The guys on the boat cheered once more as they felt the wind in their hair. It wasn't often that they were able to get away with their buddies for the weekend, and they were looking forward to doing all the things they couldn't normally do with their wives present.

This included taking a rented fishing boat as fast as it could go on the open waters.

The boat hit some choppy waves, bouncing up and down and making the men spill their beers onto the ground and seat cushions.

Diego got a little bit of beer on his new shirt, and he looked up at Kyle now, feeling pissed.

"Hey man, take it easy over there!" Diego yelled over the sound of the wind.

"Not a chance, partner," Kyle said, a big smile plastered on his face.

Diego sat back in his seat, trying to let his anger mellow down a bit. This was his boat, and he had rented it out to a group of friends for the weekend. One of the rules for renting the boat was that he had to come along on every trip for insurance purposes. If anything were to go wrong with the boat, he would be on site to fix it and ensure that his guests wouldn't be stranded in the middle of the ocean with his property. He didn't like having douchebags like these guys drive his boat, but he really needed the money. The bills were piling up, and dock fees were costly.

He didn't have many rules, but one that he insisted on was that they have the boat back at the dock by sunset. He told the guests that it was safer and easier to see where they were going, but that wasn't it at all.

The boat hit another bump, and Diego started rising to his feet again.

"Hey, guys? Maybe it's about time we start to head back. The sun is about to go down, and I don't want to be out here past sunset," Diego said. "We should start to turn..."

His words were drowned out as one of Kyle's buddies turned the knob on the stereo to full blast. The man grinned at Diego and took a sip from his beer.

Diego didn't know where the man was from, but he was pretty sure that was a sign that meant "fuck you" anywhere you went.

He turned again toward the sinking sun, and a worried look fell on his face.

If he didn't get these men under control, and get them headed back to shore soon, they wouldn't make it before the sun went down.

And if they didn't make it before the sun went down...

Diego didn't want to think about what would happen. He needed to take action now and seize control of his boat again. Was it considered a mutiny if you owned the boat?

These were the things that went through Diego's mind as he swallowed the last of his beer and made his way toward the cockpit.

One of Kyle's buddies saw Diego coming and recognized

the hostile way he was walking. The man jumped in front of him, blocking his path.

"Where do you think you're going, buddy?" the man asked, poking Diego in the chest. He was a foot taller than Diego and built like a brick house.

Diego didn't like getting pushed around, especially on his own boat. What this man didn't know was that Diego had taken several self-defense classes in his younger days.

Diego yanked on the man's wrist with one hand, twisting it behind his back, which elicited a scream from him that much higher in pitch than he was expecting. Then, with the other hand, he pressed the man's back forward, pushing his face up against one of the walls.

"I'm sorry, man. You can do whatever you want! Just let me go!" the man cried.

Diego threw the man to the side, where he fell to the ground, wincing and clutching his wrist. He walked into the cockpit, where Kyle stood staring at him dumbfoundedly.

"You can't assault us," Kyle said. "We rented this boat from you. How dare you attack my friends."

But Diego wasn't paying attention to Kyle anymore. His eyes were growing wide as he watched the sonar. A large red mass on the screen was growing closer and closer.

Diego reached for the throttle, only to be pushed away by Kyle.

"You don't understand!" Diego shouted. "You're headed straight for a..."

That was the last thing he got out before the boat rammed into a sand bank, sending everyone on board flying.

Kyle didn't know how much time had passed when he woke up. All he knew was that his head was throbbing. He brought his hand to his face, touching where it hurt, accessing the damage. His fingers came away bloody.

"Ah shit," he mumbled to himself.

He tried to stand up, but for some reason, he couldn't stand up straight. That's when he realized the boat was tilted, listing to one side as if it was about to tip over.

Are we sinking?

He looked around the deck of the boat, counting his friends. They had all been knocked out by the force of the crash and may have suffered a few concussions, but the amount of alcohol in their systems would probably save them. Fortune tended to favor the drunks.

Everyone seemed to be accounted for, except for...

Daryl? Dave?

He had forgotten the boat owner's name. He remembered thinking that it reminded him of a children's TV show, like Dora or something similar.

Had the man been thrown from the boat? Had sharks eaten him?

Just then, he heard the sound of splashing water. The sound of splashing water was constant on the ocean, but it sounded different now. It was more forceful and less like waves lapping against the boat.

Was someone drowning or...

Kyle looked over the side of the boat, where he saw Diego standing in the water.

The water level was just below his waist, so he wouldn't drown, but he seemed to be doing something underneath the surface, disrupting the dirt below and messing up the otherwise clear water around him.

"What the hell are you doing?" Kyle asked him.

Diego jumped back, seemingly shocked that there was somebody else near him.

"What does it look like I'm doing?" Diego shouted. "You crashed my boat into a sandbank, and I'm trying to dig it out!"

Kyle looked at the amount of sand around them. The sandbank was pretty large, and they wouldn't be able to get out of there anytime soon.

"You're wasting your time," Kyle said. "There's too much dirt. We'll have to get pulled out. I'll call someone over the comms system, and they should get to us in a few hours."

"We don't have a few hours!" Diego yelled, throwing another handful of dirt into the water in defeat. He looked back at the sun, which was just about to dip below the horizon. "We have to get out of here before the sun sets."

Kyle had heard the man talking about the sun all day, and he had been constantly looking back at it the whole trip.

"What's your obsession with the sunset?" Kyle asked. "Are you afraid of the dark or something?"

"You don't understand," Diego said, going for another handful of dirt. "In these waters, when the sun goes down, the monsters come out."

Kyle just shook his head at the old man. He liked coming to the islands because they always made for the best fishing trips, but he didn't have time for all the voodoo that its people believed in. He walked back to the cockpit, set on contacting the Coast Guard or whatever boat was close enough to pick him and his friends up. He would let the owner deal with his boat on his own.

He reached for the communication system, but the box was broken. It had been crushed under his weight when he flew forward during the crash. He picked up a few pieces, but it wasn't the kind of thing he knew how to fix.

Kyle decided to go with option two. He reached into his pocket, produced his cell phone, and turned it on. He also had rules for the trip, one of which was that everyone turn their phones off. The last thing they needed was a wife to call while they were on the open waters and make them have to cut the trip short. He waited while the phone booted up, then dialed emergency services, hoping to have them connect him with the Coast Guard.

But the phone wouldn't ring. He didn't have any signal.

He raised his phone in the air and walked around the boat, but the space on the screen that normally held a few bars remained empty.

They were officially stranded.

Now he was beginning to worry.

"Get down here and start helping me dig!" Diego yelled.

Kyle wasn't sure what he would do to save them, but he sure as hell wasn't going to leave the boat and jump into the water.

"Nah, I'm going to let you handle it. That's what we paid you for, right? To handle any issues that come up?" Kyle said, taking a seat in the captain's chair.

Diego looked up at the top of the boat in disbelief. *What an asshole*, he thought. His muscles were tired from digging, and he was fed up with the people who rented his boat, and to make matters worse...

Diego looked back at the sun, only moments away from disappearing behind the horizon, lighting up the sky in blazing orange hues.

There isn't enough time.

"Fuck this," Diego said, tossing down his last handful of dirt.

There was a loud splashing sound as Diego began to run along the sandbank, making his way toward the direction where he knew the shore to be. He couldn't see the shore from where he stood, but he knew he would be better off the farther he got from this spot.

Kyle heard the splashing and got up from his chair, running to the side of the boat.

"Where are you going?" he shouted to the boat's owner, but the man didn't respond; he just kept trudging along.

Diego got to the edge of the sandbank just as the sun disappeared. He dove into the water and began to swim, taking long breaststrokes as he strove to get as far away as he could.

Kyle watched as the man got farther and farther away.

He was still watching when something came up from the water beneath the man, then opened its maw wide and snatched him off the surface, dragging him into the depths where he would never be seen again.

Diego never screamed. He never made another sound. The only hint that he was ever there to begin with was the cloud of blood left behind in his wake.

"Oh my god!" Kyle yelled, and his screams were loud enough to wake several of the men on the boat, who each gave him an annoyed look as they got up.

"What's wrong?" one of the men asked, pressing a hand to the side of his head. Surprisingly, he had gone through the accident and still managed to keep a firm grip on his beer. He swirled it around in his hand, then took a sip. He nodded his head to the side and shrugged. It was a little warm, but not bad.

"It's the owner of the boat!" Kyle yelled. "He just got eaten by something under the water!"

This seemed to get the men moving, as they looked around for Diego to confirm that he was indeed missing and this wasn't a joke being played on them by their douchebag friend. They ran to the side of the boat, where Diego's blood was spreading out amongst the surface of the water as the waves lapped it up.

"Do you think it was a shark?" one of the men asked.

"That wasn't like any shark I had ever seen," Kyle said, his eyes staring at the water below, afraid to blink and miss seeing the predator that had taken Diego.

"How did he get in the water?" one of the other guys asked.

"He was trying to dig us out of the sandbank," Kyle said. "He seemed afraid of the sun setting for some reason, but why?"

Kyle looked back at where the sun had been, where darkness was beginning to take over.

What he saw chilled him to his very core.

There was a ripple in the water, coming toward them at a breakneck speed. Several others soon joined it. He couldn't see what they were, as they were still beneath the surface, but whatever they were, they would arrive in no time at all.

"Uh, guys?" Kyle asked. "I think we may be in trouble."

He didn't even get to point out the ripples to his friends before the boat was rocked like it had been hit by a train.

Some of the guys fell over, while others gripped onto the railings.

They looked over the edge, trying to see what had hit them, but they couldn't see a thing.

The boat rocked again, this time getting hit from the other direction. They didn't know what had hit them, but it was powerful.

"Hold onto something!" Kyle yelled.

They were slammed into once again, and one of his friends, who had been righting himself from the last blow, lost his footing. He took a few steps to his left before the next blow knocked him over the edge of the railing and into the waters.

Nobody moved to save him. They didn't want to leave their posts and risk falling in after him, but they heard his screams from the water.

There were a few splashes from the ocean as he made his way to the surface, and then his screams tore at their eardrums.

"No, NO, NOOO! GET AWAY FROM ME! AHH!" His screams were cut short as he was dragged into the depths.

The surviving men all looked at each other, a terrified look on their faces as they kept a white-knuckled grip on anything they could to steady themselves.

There was another loud thump as they were struck again, and this time, the boat righted itself, no longer listing to the side.

"It knocked us out of the sandbank!" Kyle said. "We can get out of here now!"

He ran over to the controls, but he wasn't fast enough.

The boat was hit once again, this time so hard that it tilted on its side, and all the men plunged into the cold waters of the ocean below.

Kyle spluttered as his mouth filled with saltwater. He opened his eyes in time to see his friends in the water around him, desperately swimming toward the surface. Unfortunately, his eyes were still open when the creatures came back around.

They were thick and muscular, covered in scales and the size of walruses. They had webbed hands with nails that ended in claws. Their faces seemed almost human, except for the gills on the sides of their throats and the fact that their mouths were like rubber, with the ability to stretch open several times larger than they should have, revealing several layers of razor-sharp teeth.

Kyle was able to make these observations as he watched the creatures pick off his friends one by one.

One of the creatures swam underneath his friend Jeremy and opened its gullet as wide as it could. It swam upward, swallowing the man's ankle, then continued up his leg until it reached his hips.

Kyle could hear Jeremy's screams even through the water and saw the look of pure terror in his eyes as the creature dragged his body down to where the sun didn't show.

His friend Alan didn't get such a pleasant fate.

Four of the creatures attacked Alan on all sides, each latching onto a different limb and crunching down at the joints. A fifth creature came and grabbed his torso, and Alan got to watch each of his limbs float away as he was taken below.

Each of the men would face similar fates, and finally, Kyle couldn't take it anymore. He needed to breathe.

He swam to the surface, taking in a breath of fresh air and feeling the tears slide down his face.

Kyle saw the last of the sun's rays turn from orange to gray, a last testament to the light he would never see again.

Then he heard a loud gurgle behind him.

Kyle turned around in the water and came face to face with one of the creatures.

It smiled at him, displaying what looked like hundreds of teeth covered in the blood of his friends.

He felt something dig into his ankles, and he was pulled under the water. He watched as the sky above him grew darker, and his vision went black.

For The Love Of Kraken

Rhiannon Lindsay-Andrews

She sits on the rock at the edge of the pool, biting her lip. She's not sure how to start, now that she's here. Is it in the water, watching her?

"Hello?" she says, tentative. *This is stupid*, she thinks. The water is completely still. There's nothing there.

"Good afternoon," comes a gentle voice in her head, lapping at the edge of her thoughts as if asking permission to enter. It's as soft as waves kissing her toes.

"Hi," she says. There's something here, at least, so she's not a total fool. "I'm Eliza. It's nice to meet you."

"Eliza," repeats the voice, and it's like she can hear it tasting her name. This is an audition for both of them, and if she doesn't make a good impression, she won't be invited back. *Do you know what I am, Eliza?*

"I do," she says, her voice quiet, and she clears her throat before trying again. "I do."

There's a long pause, and when the voice comes again, it sounds amused. *"And what is that, dear one?"*

She clears her throat again. Somehow it's harder to say out loud now, even though she's been trying for days. Ever since she made this appointment. "A Kraken."

No, it says again, and this time it definitely sounds amused, like it's laughing at her. *"I am THE Kraken. There is no other."*

"Of course," she says, blushing. "I'm sorry."

A thin black tentacle pushes its way out of the water, stopping by her foot. *It's immaterial,* the voice says. *"Why are you here, Eliza?"*

She stares at the tentacle. She's trying very hard not to think it looks rather small, rather thin, and she certainly doesn't wonder what good it would be. "I made an appointment," she says, blushing.

Yes, the voice says. It sounds almost impatient, and she knows she needs to do better. Needs to be able to answer its questions without blushing, but she flinches when the tentacle touches her bare ankle. It's cold and wet, and recoils instantly from her.

"Are you scared, dear one? You can leave, if this is too much."

"No!" she says. Too fast. "No, this isn't too much. I'm just... nervous, I guess. I haven't done this before."

The tentacle touches her ankle again, and this time she doesn't flinch. It caresses her skin, inching its way up, and when she shudders, it's with anticipation instead of fear.

"Tell me why you're here, Eliza." There's a note of command in its voice, and she can't refuse.

"I want you," she whispers. "I heard about you being here, and I haven't been able to stop thinking about you. I want—" She cuts herself off, blushing, and the tentacle curls around her knee and stays there, softly teasing the back of it and making her shudder again.

Tell me, and she's not sure how a voice in her head can whisper. She shakes her head, so the voice continues, *"Very well. What can you tell me?"*

She takes a moment to breathe, to decide. "I like you touching me," she says, and she hears its smile in her head. She feels bold. "I want to touch you."

"Not this time, dear one", it says. *"For now, I'd like to know more about you."* Another tentacle appears from the water, reaching for her other ankle, and she's suddenly viciously glad she wore a skirt. The tentacles stay below her knee, teasing, and she wants more.

"What do you want to know?" she asks, and she can hear the almost-whine in her voice as she shifts, trying to encourage the tentacles higher.

"Patience," the voice chides, but it rewards her by moving up slightly, to mid-thigh, still far too low for her liking. She hasn't been touched like this in months, not since her ex, and it feels like every second has been leading up to this. To make her want this. *"Eliza, do you like when I do this?"*

A third tentacle comes out of the pool, snaking up her body and grasping her wrist. It tightens just enough that she can feel it, and she nods eagerly. *"Use your words, Eliza. This won't work without that."*

"Yes," she says, amazed that she can sound so together, and when a fourth tentacle wraps around her other wrist, pulling both her arms back ever so slightly, she lets out a shaky breath. Need rises in her, a slow drip that, if she had more of her brain for thought, would make her laugh with the irony. The first two tentacles leave her legs, moving up, and they hover above the buttons of her dress. "Yes," she says again before the Kraken can ask, and they lower gently, unbuttoning her, exposing her to the warm sun.

They don't touch her, not yet, and the grip on her wrists loosens slightly. *"Eliza, are you certain? Do you want this?"* The voice sounds almost anxious, and she nods before it's finished speaking.

"Yes, I want this. I want you," she says, and she's never been more sure of anything. This is better than her dreams, and when the tentacles clasp her wrists again, she sighs with pleasure.

The others softly graze her breasts, and they're slightly cold and damp. The tip of one of them flicks her left nipple, with all the promise of pain. She can't believe she thought of her ex. Nothing was like this with him. It was perfunctory, never about her and what she might enjoy, and it took months before she realised there was something to miss.

She's brought back to the present when the Kraken presses the tip of a tentacle on her lips, the weight pulling her jaw down and opening her mouth. She wants to taste the tentacle, feel it inside her mouth, but it stays carefully on her bottom lip.

"What distracts you, Eliza? Are my attentions not what you hoped for?" There's a tinge beneath the calm words that she wants to believe is apprehension. Is she thinking into this too much? Does it want her, or is it just fulfilling an obligation?

"Sorry," she says. "I was just... I haven't got much experience of... well, anything." She blushes yet again, and immediately regrets her words when all of the tentacles move from her skin.

"You are... You have not been touched before?" the voice says, sounding alarmed. *"They did not tell me that you were so."*

She moves, following the tentacles as they slide back into the water. "NO!" Her voice is loud, surprising herself, and the tentacles stop. "No, I have been touched. It just wasn't very good." She would feel embarrassed saying this to another person, but somehow the facelessness of the Kraken makes it easier for her to be honest. The lake can't look horrified, and she senses no judgement in the tentacles that start sliding back to her. She doesn't feel the urge to cover herself. She wants to be open. "I've never...finished," she says, hearing the weakness of her words, but she doesn't feel comfortable using the vulgarity her sister prefers.

The tentacles guide her back to the rock she was sitting on before, their gentleness a complete contrast to the anger she hears as the Kraken says, *"Forgive me for asking such a base question, but I would like to be explicit here. Are you saying you've never had an orgasm at the touch of your partner? That they didn't bother to do so?"*

She shakes her head before remembering the Kraken's earlier request to use her words. "No. He would finish, but there never seemed to be time for more than that, and I..." She trails off, not sure how to phrase it.

The Kraken seems to understand her, thankfully. *"My darling Eliza, you should not have had to ask your partner to spend time pleasuring you, unless that was agreed beforehand. The fact that this man did not care enough to pleasure you, that he did not appreciate your radiant beauty, is intolerable. What kind of fool, what bastard, what abstract disaster of a human is he?"*

The voice grows louder and louder in Eliza's head, and not even the gentle caresses of the tentacles on her ankles are enough to stop her from wincing. The tentacles stop moving immediately, the voice going deadly quiet.

"Sorry," she says, tapping her temple. "You were just a little loud."

"My apologies."

The Kraken finally moves its tentacles up her legs again, the movement soft and teasing, and one of the tentacles rubs at her temple, easing the tension there. The tip of one tentacle draws lazy circles on her upper thigh, every trip around bringing it closer to the apex of her legs, and she's so distracted by this that she almost misses the Kraken's next words. *"So, what made you decide I should be the one to first bring you to your peak? I am honoured, of course, but intrigued. Why not find a less useless human?"*

"I didn't want a human," she says, her voice thick with desire, and she's almost certain she hears a groan in her head. Can something groan if it doesn't have vocal cords? A tentacle slowly circles her neck, another binding her wrists together, a third trailing over her nipples with a featherlight touch that makes her arch into it, a fourth so close to her clitoris that she can taste her own need, she wonders how someone could want anything but this.

The tentacle around her neck flexes, squeezing just a little, and she swallows in anticipation, her eyes closing. The lake bubbles as if something is moving, and she wonders if she could persuade the Kraken to surface. If she can be its first customer to see it. *"Do you want me?"* The voice says, and she nods. *"Your words, sweetling."*

"Yes," she says, almost interrupting. "Yes, I want you."

"Shall we see how sweet you really are?" The Kraken asks,

and she gasps as the tip of one tentacle carefully circles the bundle of nerves that aches for attention. The Kraken is deliberate in its movements, and she doesn't notice the other tentacle until it's touching her opening. It feels thicker, and it dips into her centre, pushing in just enough for her to feel it before retreating again. She opens her eyes again in time to see this new appendage dipping back into the water. As it comes out again and heads back towards her, the Kraken speaks, the words lower in tone. *"Delicious"*, it says, and then she's full of it.

It is warm and slick, stretching her, and she is being moved so that it can reach every millimetre of her. There is pressure on her clit, a sucker she hadn't noticed pulling at the nerves and making her clench around the tentacle inside her. *This*, she thinks, *is exactly what I needed.*

"Yes, sweetling," the Kraken replies, and of course it can hear her thoughts. She's not sure why she's surprised. *"Relax for me."*

She can't. Her every muscle is tense as the pressure builds, her legs shaking as the Kraken holds her up and in position, her breath coming in gasps, and just as it gets too much, as the scales tip ever closer to pain, her stomach tensing as it tries to curl into itself, to force her into a foetal position, the shackles tighten, and the denial makes the sensations stronger.

The tentacle stays inside as she pulses around it, but the sucker that had been lavishing attention on her clit retreats too soon, and she gasps. "Please," she begs, not certain what she's asking for but knowing she needs something. *Please*, she thinks, hoping it can tell what she wants from the blur of her thoughts.

It touches her again, and she relaxes into the rock, into the brief respite. She can feel the pressure again, somewhere deep inside her, but she takes a second to catch her breath, to remember her manners. "Thank you," she says, and she hears the Kraken laugh, feels the tremors inside her as it shakes with amusement.

"You do not need to thank me, precious. It was all my pleasure," the voice says, and she hesitates for barely a second.

"Was it? Really? I want..." She pauses, trying to take a deep breath as the tentacle inside her shifts, twisting. She wonders if it's deliberately distracting her. "More," she breathes out, more gasp than word.

"More? What more is there?" The voice asks, gentle and teasing. It wants her to say it. Her words fail her as her breath speeds up, and she instead thinks of the image she saw years ago, a fantasy that stuck with her. *"Like that?"* the Kraken says, and she hears the water move as another tentacle joins her on the rock.

"How did that bastard not appreciate this jewel?" She's not sure she's meant to have heard that last sentence, the words so quiet they barely enter her mind, but as the new tentacle, easily as thick as the one that gently pulses inside her, touches her bottom lip, she forgets it. She opens her mouth, and as she tastes the salt on

her tongue, she remembers when her ex would do this, demanding participation. The Kraken fills her, uses her, and as her second orgasm builds in her, she runs her tongue down the underside of the tentacle, feeling the way it shudders against her, and she hears the water ripple again. *"You are a danger"*, the voice says, or maybe it says, *"You are in danger."* She's not sure what she prefers.

She's lost track of where she is, only conscious of where she is filled, and her next orgasm rips through her, almost making her choke with the force of it. She's so close to what she wants, and as she tries to recover, mouth still full, she wonders how to word her request. *I want you*, she begins, and she hears the smile in her head. *All of you.*

"You have all of me", it replies, almost chiding. Almost, but she can hear the desire in its words, and she knows she can override the Kraken's refusals.

"Any more and this would not end well for you."

Please, she thinks, and she wonders if it has the same begging tenor that she wants it to have. *I know what will happen. I'm ready. Please.*

There is a long pause, and when the Kraken breaks it, she knows she's won. *You know what will happen and you still desire it? Still desire me?*

Yes, she says, repeating it over and over again. *Yes yes yes yes yes yes*. It is a litany, a prayer, and when she hears the water rumble, when the tentacles retreat from her throat and cunt, when the restraints release and allow her to move again, when she is all but free in case she wants to run, she smiles.

She opens her eyes just in time to see the hulking mass rise from the water. It's bigger than she had thought, and her smile grows. She sees the head, rising out of the water, more eyes than skin, and it is ten eleven twelve feet out of the water, still more submerged, and she's proud of how there isn't even a flicker of fear. This is it—the promised death.

"Yes," she says, anticipating its question of whether she's sure. She's shadowed by it, only the tips of tentacles still in the water now, and she can see the full horror of the Kraken as it approaches her. It reaches for her, lifting her gently around the waist, and as it pulls her closer, she can see the daggers still stuck into it from where people tried to defend themselves against it. She can't understand why they would want to. She's pulled closer, into the tangle of tentacles, into the heart of it, and the heat of them is immense. She's almost certain she sees a bone in a crevice of skin, but she ignores it. She doesn't want to think of the Kraken's ex-lovers right now.

There is a tentacle in the middle, the thickest, and she knows this is what is going to ruin her. Her breath is shaky, and she feels her need trickle down her thigh. She focuses on that, trying to direct the sensation at the Kraken, making sure it can tell she is desperate for this. She is held, suspended by her ankles and wrists, tentacles encircling her forearms and calves, putting her in the position she will die in. Sweat beads down her spine as the press of tentacles grows, and she pants as the Kraken begins to move the central tentacle.

"Are you certain?" It asks, desire making the voice thick in her head, the thin note of anxiety disappearing as she replies.

I have wanted this my whole life. I need you. Please. The words are calm, considering how her muscles tremble with anticipation, and as it slowly touches her, she takes one last deep breath.

It doesn't hurt at first. It feels like the other tentacles had, and two smaller ones hover beside the main one, delicately holding her open. It's only as it gets too big and starts to push harder, demanding more room, demanding to fill her beyond capacity, that she wonders if she should regret this. A fleeting thought, one she doesn't have time for, not when her legs are being pulled apart, more literally than any human could have ever managed. The Kraken, all anxiety gone, fills her head with thoughts of how many times it has done this, how grateful it is, how it honours her sacrifice.

Her last thought, as she is cleaved in two, split open by the Kraken's desire, is that it isn't fair she has to die to achieve true pleasure.

Charlotte Montgomery is, as are most millennials, tired. Irish, but living in Scotland, Charlotte spends most of her free time writing, watching mindless television, or listening to a motley collection of bubblegum pop and trap music.

A Sinking Feeling

Danna Greenwood

At midnight the pier was empty, the light from the lampposts dulled by the swirling fog. A woman in a black trench coat walked along the dock, her head down and hands in her pockets. Salty air misted around her as she stumbled, tripping over a raised plank, then carrying on.

She pulled a flask out of her coat and took a swig, continuing down the pier until she found a bench to sit on. Everything was still for several moments as the fog thickened, curling around her ankles.

Today had been one of her worst days. One thing after another kept coming her way without reprieve, and she wasn't sure she could deal with it anymore. She was nauseous and had a migraine. It was never going to get better, and today she finally realized the extent of her bleakness – the pregnancy test had been positive.

The woman stood up and climbed on the bench, peering over the railing edge. Black water swirled below as the waves hit the pilings in a hypnotic rhythm; the woman swayed back and forth matching the ebb and flow of the ocean.

She took a deep breath and screamed into the night. The primal roar reached across the sea, some of it absorbed by the fog, while some found its way to the farthest reaches of the ocean's depths. She released all the anger and frustration that had built up over the last few weeks.

Peering into the chaos of the water, the woman felt dizzy and unhinged, like everything and nothing was possible in the universe. She pulled out the flask and threw it into the water, tears running down her face.

Her head in her hands, trembling in the cold, she felt so tired. A breeze blew her hair across her face, and the salt spray made her face feel grimy. She heard a low hum coming from the sea. The woman looked across the water and the seawater shimmered.

A song floated through the air. The lullaby was soothing, calming her nerves and warming her insides. The song spoke to her, telling her how things would be different if she went into the water. It would cleanse her of her past wrongdoings.

She heard a splashing noise and peered over the balustrade. A flash of something white bobbed to the surface of the seawater and disappeared again into the waves.

The woman braced one arm on the railing and one arm on the

lamppost, lifting herself up.

"Wait," a voice called.

A figure emerged from the haze, his face obscured by the shadows, standing on the opposite side of the pier.

The woman paused, one leg up on the railing and one leg on the bench. "Leave me alone."

"Come on, there's got to be something worth living for. It's not all bad, right?" His eyes glowed in the dark.

"Go away, creep." The woman lifted the other leg up onto the railing and found her balance.

"Life is funny sometimes. There are ups and downs," he said. "The pain will pass, I promise. Then you will get to experience the beauty of life."

"Shut up, mister," the woman said. "You don't know what you are talking about."

The man stepped closer. "Let me help—"

The woman jumped, free-falling for a few moments before her body hit the water. She expected it to be cold, but the water was warm—like when her mom had bathed her when she was young.

She sank, the currents pulling and pushing her trench coat in different directions. There was darkness all around her, but with the next wave, she saw a blur of white and swam towards it. She reached out and wrapped her hands around the object.

It was a tiny skeleton, small enough to belong to a baby. She held the bones close to her chest and felt a sharp pain in her abdomen. She bent over in pain and screamed, releasing bubbles to the surface. Her body spasmed for a few seconds, then went limp.

She was in the middle of a sunny field, the sound of a child's laughter filling the air. A small, warm hand grabbed hers and tugged, pulling her towards a playground.

Next, she was in a dark room that smelled of milk and baby powder, swaying back and forth in a rocking chair. A warm, heavy weight slept on her chest, rising, and falling with each breath. The nightlight shaped as a baby elephant plugged in the corner emitted a comforting glow.

She was at the zoo, pointing out animals and pushing a stroller. Wiping off sticky ice cream from cheeks and fingers.

The woman was at the beach, lathering on sunscreen, pulling a hat tight onto a tiny head, brushing sand off tiny toes. Chubby legs waddled towards the waves.

She felt an immense joy and light surround her; she kicked her legs to get back to the surface. Her body was filled with strength and life she had never known before.

The woman blinked, suddenly back on the pier, the wooden planks beneath her feet. The dock was empty, the fog swirling around the lampposts. Her coat was dry as if she had never gone into the water. The man was no longer there. She looked down at the dark water down below; the waves had calmed, and the water gently lapped against the pilings.

She put her hand on her stomach and felt a flutter. Smiling, she walked back down the pier to her car.

Behind her, at the end of the dock, eyes glowed through the fog. The man hummed a lullaby as he jumped off the pier and disappeared into the sea.

Danna Greenwood is an author of short stories and essays. Her horror short stories have appeared in Scare Street: Night Terrors and Blood-Soaked Pages. When she's not writing, Danna watches scary movies, reads creepy books, and goes on walks with her two furbabies. Danna lives in Huntsville, Alabama. Follow her on X: @DannaAuthor and IG: @ dannaauthor.

Epitaph For A Whaleman

Susan E. Rogers

The Stones.

I flip away the strands of my long hair to finger the heart-shaped locket at my throat, a treasure found washed up on the beach after November's nor'easter. Inside, a young man's miniature, barely beard enough to shave, smiles opposite a tawny curl. To Mother, Love from Your Jack smeared on thick, yellowed paper. His identity lures me here, relinquished at long last after six months searching.

A low wall surrounds the graveyard, crafted with skill and dignity. Where intact, the façade is flat, pieces meticulously fit to the smoothness of veneer. Time demands its due, though. Greenish-gray moss floods into crevices, seeps into seams, and releases bonds of rock fitted to rock. Jagged points of dried maple leaf poke from cracks like harpoon barbs. Cascades of loosened stone splash down either side, onto the sidewalk at street's edge and inwards onto swells of grass along its backside.

Entranced though I am, these stones don't tempt me to linger.

The opening in the wall faces the Bunker lot, the rusted iron stile no longer a barrier. Silence oozes its tendrils through my senses, pine needles noiseless beneath my step. There to the right, three graves rest together. A thrum of energy floods my ears as I approach, fingertips tingling.

I whisper the names—Elizabeth slightly apart, John Sr. in the middle, and John Jr., my Jack, on the left. His stone leans toward his father's, nearly touching, consoling. A long, shallow crack crosses the face, yet the weather-worn carving remains legible.

I reach to grasp the top of Jack's gravestone. A vibrating jolt gushes up my arm, intense without pain or trauma. Affixed to the slab, rough grain caresses my palm, cool and soothing. My lips murmur his name to the stone again and again. I close my eyes and let Jack flow into me. The image of a young sailor meets my stare, cocksure gleam in his eye.

The Sea

No wind for days. Sails drape like shrouds from the skeleton of masts, festooned with cobwebs of idle rope. The ship drifts where the current takes her, these windless doldrums our unrelenting nemesis. Impotent waves ripple across a sea as smooth as silk and lap softly against the hull. My crew is colorblind to all but tones of blue. Water gleams like gunmetal. A cloudless sky so blue-hot it sears eyeballs without a shade.

Forty leagues from the tip of New Zealand's North Island and no sighting of ship nor beast for three weeks. The holds are empty of oil, save for two hundred barrels taken from one humpback near the Galapagos. A sad portion of the two thousand needed for full, and it must be traded for provisions at the next port, when that shall ever be. Shares will be poor for those invested in this voyage, perhaps none at all for the crew.

Captain Butler speaks of omens. A shark seen trailing the ship a fortnight ago. Whispers of a Jonah on board trickle through the crew's quarters at night when the grog is downed and tongues are free. The men report a greenhand gone overboard last evening, not yet sixteen years. Homesick, they tell the captain, gone mad from these endless days of blue. They spit in their hands and whistle to the wind.

I sit with a half-written letter to my father. This voyage has seen two years and still the prize remains elusive.

Dearest Father. I pray this letter finds you and Mother in good health... Our voyage has not been over fortunate. As First Mate, I embrace my duty to set an example for the crew and I bear these misfortunes with manly fortitude...

I wake to a rocking bunk and raucous shouts from above. The bosun's whistle shrills. I scramble to the deck and look out into the night. A quarter moon offers light enough to see black silhouette on dark, a fluke's undulation and silvery spray in the air.

The Storm

My father will be glad of the letter sent to him by packet boat from Savannah these few days ago, proud at the news that First Mate's success is finally mine. Thirty months out and home is but two days' sail to New Bedford, holds brimming with precious oil, the inauspicious start to this voyage negated by unexpected windfall over the past half year. A shudder drips down my spine as I stand on deck to watch dawn's light douse the sky in crimson. In the shadowed clouds, I see the face of the lad sacrificed to the sea six months this day.

Red sky in morning, sailors take warning.

Winds freshen through the hours. Sunset sky is bruised to yellowing shades of purple. Seething black clouds stalk us from the south. By nightfall, angry gusts rile the waves and pummel the listing ship. Montauk's beach beckons through a veil of driven rain. Masts sway and timbers quake. The ship becomes a sickening seesaw, threatening to retch its cargo.

Salt-laden ropes grind against davits slick with rain. Eight of us, holding fast to braces, prepare to drop into the churning mass of sea below. The whaleboat lowers, pitching and swinging, toward its insatiable maw. We hit the water. A wave ten times our height snatches us in its grasp and hurls us with the strength of Poseidon back down to the sea's boiling surface. The whaleboat breaks in two with an ear-splitting crack.

I fly, then crash through the sea's craggy skin, sinking into the green frothing current that flings me about like a broken marionette. I free myself from lengths of writhing rope but can make no progress toward the surface. My lungs beg for sweet air. William looms before me, thrashing to free himself from the serpentine sail. I reach out to pull the coiling cloth away. His arms wave too wildly and my fingers are too cold. The sail and William plummet past me, their wake hauling me after them. The sodden wool of my heavy peacoat weights me like ballast stones, and I plunge toward the depths of no return.

One last effort to swim upward, and my blurry eyes behold a woman's face. Her unfamiliar voice breathes my name, and my lips curl in a rictus grin to welcome her.

The Surrender

Waves of seething energy stream from the gravestone and their undertow grips my fingers, wrenching me from the stone into watery darkness. My hair splays around my head, becoming a funereal wreath as I'm dragged deep beneath the savage surf. My breath catches in my throat, lungs sucking inward to the risk of collapse as they fill with brine. My arms flail, my eyes bulge as Jack's spectral face, mouth wide, leans toward me. One hand rips the locket from my throat, his other reaches behind my neck and pulls me close for a ghostly kiss as he draws the final breaths from my body. I resist at first, but with no success. The locket floats to the surface, my last vision, a lure for Jack's next victim.

In Memory

John Bunker Jr.

First Mate of Bark Plato

Lost at Sea

October 15, 1842

Susan E. Rogers lives in sunny St. Pete Beach, Florida, USA transplanted from Massachusetts. Her move was the catalyst to focus on her life-long ambition to write. Her other interests include genealogy and psychic spirituality, and she often twists these into her writing. She self-published her first book in 2018 about her own psychic experiences, and published an occult thriller with an indie press in Sept. 2023. A supernatural mystery novel is under contract with another publisher for a planned release in 2024. Starting in 2020, her short fiction has been published in print anthologies and several literary and genre magazines, including Cobra Milk Literary, Bluing the Blade, Luna Station Quarterly, Nightmare Narratives, and Horror Tree's Trembling with Fear.

Dr. Marie Lestrange is a multipassionate badass that plays eight musical instruments and is deathly afraid of chickens. She's the author of the gothic historical novel *Crimson Cobblestones* and hosts a weekly indie Horror podcast called Moths to the Flame. She's obsessed with research into the macabre, true crime, and occultish practices and is also the founding chairman of the Horror Writers Association Tennessee Chapter. When not writing, she and her writer husband, Bert, love traveling with their little Hobbit outside of the East Tennessee mountains they call home. **Links:** https://linktr.ee/lestrangebooks

Want More From The

SINISTER SOCIETY?

Follow along on our social media accounts
@sinistersociety

&

Join our Facebook Group for submissions
calls and latest updates!
https://www.facebook.com/groups/1444531013102495